Ballet of Bullets

The Game Is Dodging Death

By Jerry Bader

MRPwebmedia.com/books
Amazon.com/author/jerrybader

Ballet of Bullets

The Game Is Dodging Death

Written by Jerry Bader

Illustrations by Paola Ceccantoni

ISBN Paperback: 978-1-988647-62-3
Hard Cover: 978-1-988647-63-0
Ebook: 978-1-988647-64-7

"WE'RE NOT IN KANSAS ANYMORE"

1
"Toto, I've a feeling
we're not in Kansas anymore."
The Wizard of Oz, 1939

Benny Silver is used to being uncomfortable, but this is different; different from the times he sat across the desk from his boss who complained that if Jews were so smart why was he so fucking dumb; different from the time he went to his buddy's Catholic wedding where he was sure the priest was going to force him to drop his pants to see if he was circumcised; and different from the time he went to that specialist whose office was covered in crosses and giant photographs of bearded Coptic priests. This is very different; this is bat-shit crazy.

The temperature in the church had to be a hundred and ten degrees. The sweat beaded on the foreheads of the inmates of this over-crowded fundamentalist asylum like poison pustules being excoriated by God, cleansing the evil spirits from their depraved craven bodies. Older women fanned themselves with paper fans bought at the local dollar store, all the while bitching to the Latino cashier of the lack of a good Woolworth that used to carry the good ones. The men in their cream-colored suits mopped their brows with white linen handkerchiefs. Most had stripped down to their white short-sleeve Wal-

Mart specials accented by hideous extra wide ties left over from the fifties and sixties.

Benny in his dark navy blue Armani and imported red silk Battistoni tie wasn't the only big city blot on this otherwise uniformly rural backwater enclave. Sitting in the second row in a position of honor is Walter Cummings Gordon, Chairman of the Board of InfoSilo Corporation, a major player in invading the personal lives of a naïve and oblivious public, more interested in posting baby bump pictures online than protecting their right to privacy. Beside him sits his dried up prune of a wife, Martha Carter Gordon and his ne'er-do-well asshole son, Freddy, fresh from his latest round of rehab intended to purge his fixation with gambling, pharmaceuticals, and women of moral ambiguity. It is the senior Gordon that brought Benny to this Southern cultural-shock of an experience. Meanwhile, the overstuffed preacher carried on about various excesses of which he appeared to be a firsthand expert.

The preacher stomps his foot in a dramatic effort to wake the dead. He raises one elephantine arm to the sky and the other to his ear, "Can I hear an Amen?" Several members of the congregation respond to his demand with random shouts of "Amen!" The Preacher stalks his flock like a hyena zoning in on the weak and vulnerable, ready to pounce on a victim at the slightest whiff of fear, insecurity, or guilt.

"Praise Jesus!" He stomps his foot again demanding attention, "There are many so-called religions in this world and they all say they believe in God; but I ask you: do they really? Do they really believe in the one true God, Praise Jesus!" Multiple shouts from the congregation erupt in a chorus of "NO!" and "Hell No!"

Preacher: "Amen Brother, Amen!" He pauses to scout the overheated parishioners for his next victim. He spots his prey, an anemic female soul in an aisle seat. He bends his gargantuan body so that the rolls of fat bunch up in a mountain of blubber; his foul sweat is held back only by the thinnest of cheap Chinese workmanship mercifully protecting the poor woman from a horrible death by cellulite asphyxiation. He leans in close so the woman can capture the faintest lingering aroma of his pre-worship Jack Daniels.

Preacher: "Have you ever sent your man for milk?" The woman nods reluctantly. "That's okay my dear, there's no sin in that. We've all gone to the store to get some milk. Now when I was a boy it was easy, you went and bought milk. Today, it's not so simple. Today... it's downright perplexing, mystifying, and thoroughly confusing. The last time I went to the Piggly Wiggly I counted how many different kinds of milk they had. Twenty-five. Can you imagine twenty-five different kinds of milk? They got one percent, two percent, three percent, five percent..." He pauses..."I asked the lad what happened to the four percent, and you know what he told me? He told me it was back-ordered." The congregation laughs.

The preacher makes his way back down the aisle to the front of the congregation. "They got chocolate milk and strawberry milk, and almond milk, and goat milk, and it all comes in multiple fat content options. So, my friends, you understand my point. I don't want no one percent soy concoction on my corn flakes. I don't want no two percent almond goat fabrication in my coffee. I don't want a glass of watery imitation pretend-milk with my roast beef sandwich."

Benny almost throws up in his mouth at the thought of drinking milk with a roast beef sandwich. He thinks to himself they probably even butter the Wonder Bread. He laughs. The preacher spots Benny and points a giant sausage-sized finger in his direction. "Amen Brother! I don't want your pseudo milk, your imitation wannabe milk. I don't want no fake milk... and I, sure as God made little green apples, don't want no false Gods. Give me the real thing. PRAISE JESUS! Do I Hear An Amen!" And the congregation all shouts AMEN! On cue, they burst into a chorus of "Amazing Grace." Even Benny was ready to thank God... thank God it was over. Now he could get down to business.

THE LIMO RIDE

2
The Limo Ride

With the service over, Benny makes his way outside to wait for the Gordons. The preacher stands
by the door blocking half of it with his massive
bulk forcing well-wishers to navigate around him
and onto the church steps where he can look
down upon them like the almighty vessel of the
truth he professes to be. As Benny watches, he
sees Walter Gordon exit the church. Gordon
shakes the preacher's massive ham-sized paw
while exchanging pleasantries. Gordon points to
Benny. The preacher motions for Benny to come
over. Benny reluctantly makes his way up the
church steps to the rung below Gordon and two
rungs below the preacher.

Preacher: "Did you enjoy the service son?"

Benny doesn't quite know what to say, "It certainly was a new experience."

Preacher: "I get a distinctly Old Testament air
about you boy. Are you a believer?"

Benny: "Well sir, I believe in all sorts of things."

Preacher: "But do you believe in the one true
God? Do you believe in Jesus Christ?"

Benny is just about ready to tell this lard-ass southern cracker exactly what he believes in, but he thinks better of it. There is just too much money on the line. And he has no intention of fucking up this deal over some religious crackpot who equates God to buying milk. "With all due respect sir, I take my coffee black."

Gordon's son Freddy who's standing in front of his mother but behind his father smirks, "Amen brother!" At which point Walter Gordon has heard enough. He practically pushes Benny off the steps making his way to the waiting limousine and driver.

Benny: "Shall I follow you to the club, Mr. Gordon? My renter is just over there."

Gordon: "No you can come with us in the limo. We can conclude our business on the way to the club and my driver will bring you back here when we're done."

Benny: "I see... I thought we were going to have lunch at your club and conclude our business there?"

Gordon: "I'm afraid the club doesn't allow out-of-town guests on Sunday, so lunch would be impossible. I'm sure you understand."

Benny understands all too well, "Sure Mr. Gordon I understand exactly. Your club is restricted. I wouldn't want you to get a letter of reprimand from the board."

Gordon: "No need to be sarcastic Mr. Silver, this is the South and we have our ways. When in Rome and so forth..." His words trail off as they reach the limo. Benny tells Gordon he has to retrieve the paperwork from his car. By the time he returns the Gordons have stuffed themselves into the front-facing back seat, leaving the back-facing bench free for Benny to occupy all by himself: they obviously didn't want any Old Testament contamination to leak all over their newly invigorated spiritual fortification.

Freddy is arguing with his father. "You shouldn't be selling it. It's a mistake. Suarez says it can be a big money maker. I can run it if you want to keep your hands clean. You worry too fucking much about what that religious charlatan thinks."

Martha: "Shut your foul mouth and don't be telling your father what to do. That Mexican bandit is no friend of ours, and I certainly don't want you to have anything to do with him or this whole unsavory enterprise."

Freddy: "First of all, he's Peruvian, not Mexican, and he's not a bandit he's a businessman. He was an astronaut for Christ's sake."

Martha: "You idiot! *El Astronauta* is a nickname taken from the Nazca geoglyphs. Maybe if you finished school, you'd know what you're talking about. And what about that ape of a Chinaman, Tommy Kong? He follows your pal around like some giant oversized shadow? Don't tell me he's a businessman with all those tattoos."

Freddy: "So you rather sell it to the Jew-boy here. Suarez will make you a better offer."

Gordon: "SHUT UP! Both of you, shut up. The business is already sold, and it's not to Mr. Silver, so you both can just shut up and let me complete my business. I'm still the President of the company and I still intend to get paid during the transition."

Freddy points to Benny, "So what's he doing here?"

Gordon: "Mr. Silver is a television executive. And he's here to sign a contract to have the tournaments televised throughout the entire WSN Broadcast System. InfoSilo will be sponsoring the whole deal." Benny hands Gordon a black leather legal-sized folio filled with various documents. Gordon signs the documents and hands them back to Benny. The limo pulls into the circular driveway that fronts the neoclassical antebellum Spicebush Golf and Country Club. Freddy is pissed. He doesn't even wait for the limo to come to a complete stop before he opens the door to leave, but his mother reaches across him and grabs the handle slamming it shut.

Martha: "Wait for your father you little shit. And don't embarrass us in front of our friends."

Gordon looks at Benny. "My driver will take you back to the church so you can pick up your car. I expect to receive my monthly compensation as usual for the next six months, but I'll no longer be going to the office. I assume you or Mr. Stone have already made arrangements for someone new to take my place." Benny nods.

Gordon, his wife, and son get out of the limo and head for the entrance to the Spicebush Golf and Country Club's main building. As the limo pulls around the circular driveway heading towards the exit Benny hears what sounds like firecrackers, but they're not; they're gunshots. He moves to the back window and sees one of the gardeners running towards the road as Martha Gordon kneels beside her dead husband and wounded son. The limo driver slams on the brakes. He turns to see what's happened.

Benny: "Don't stop! Get us the hell out of here."

Driver: "But Mr. Gordon..."

Benny: "Fuck that racist asshole. There may be more shooting. Get us out of here now!" The driver hits the accelerator as all hell breaks loose behind them.

EVERYTHING IS A POTENTIAL BET

3
Everything Is A Potential Bet

Gamblers are not a particularly choosy bunch;
they'll bet on anything: horses, dogs, cocks, and
even people, and that's the dumbest bet of all.
You can juice an animal to run fast, run slow, and
ignore pain, but if that horse, dog, camel, or fight-
ing kangaroo just doesn't feel like cooperating,
you're fucked. Fixing a horserace is complicated
because you have to deal with the horse, multiple
jockeys, and maybe the trainer, vet, and owner.
It's messy, and more than likely, someone in the
chain of degenerates will screw up or go rogue,
but that doesn't stop people from trying.

People will bet on anything from over/under to
the color of stool a horse drops before a big race.
Everything is a goddamn competition; everything
is a potential bet. Benny remembers his Uncle Sol
taking him to the ball games when he was a kid.
Sol didn't give a shit about baseball, what he
liked was being with his cronies, betting on
everything from who'd get the next hit to how
many times the batter would scratch his balls before he got into the batter's box. As long as people are stupid enough to bet, they'll be others eager to take their money; and that is the business
of the Hancock Entertainment Corporation.

If dummies are prepared to throw their hard-
earned cash away, the Hancock is eager to pro-

vide the means for them to do it with an inte-
grated network of racetracks, casinos, and gambling clubs. It is the reason Johnny Luck, CEO of
the Hancock, had his protégé, Jesse James, get
her husband, William Stone, to buy the International Jai Alai League from Walter Cummings Gordon for fifty million dollars.

The league already operated *frontons* in Miami,
Atlantic City, Las Vegas, and Reno. Stone and his
Hancock associates envisioned expanding inter-
nationally making the IJAL truly international by
opening frontons in Los Angeles, Crystal Beach,
Canada, Tijuana, Mexico, and eventually Palermo,
Argentina where they operated racetracks with
pari-mutuel wagering already in place. Racetracks cannot survive on racing alone; they need
slot machines, casino games, and whatever else
that can be added to turn them into gambling
theme parks; and so, Jai Alai is resurrected from
the ash heap of alternative sporting events.

Walter Gordon was desperate to unload the Jai
Alai operation despite the fact it was a substantial money maker. The whiff of gambling and for-
eigners that barely spoke *American* made his fellow southern bible thumpers nervous, not to
mention InfoSilo stockholders and the Securities
and Exchange Commission. If Gordon was involved in gambling; sex, and drugs, then rock-
and-roll would not be far behind. Gordon's golf-
ing buddies may have viewed his Jai Alai business dealings with a jaundiced eye, but their

parochial impression was not far off the mark. In recent months it had become clear that the Miami fronton had been infiltrated by a Peruvian drug dealer, Marco Antonio Suarez, nicknamed *El Astronauta,* and his three-hundred-pound, shaved-head partner with the massive white Fu Manchu mustache, Tommy The King Kong.

Suarez and Kong installed half a dozen gamblers in the Miami fronton. These gamblers controlled the betting in the fronton through a series of payoffs to the official handicapper who produced the game-day tout sheet for bettors; the pari-mutuel manager who supplied computer print-outs of pre-match betting numbers; and key players. In some cases, fronton employees made more money with bribes than they received in their weekly paychecks. Any player or fronton employee that didn't cooperate found the brakes in their car mysteriously stopped working. When the second-ranking singles player, Xavier Gebara, refused to throw a match, he ended-up wrapping his Audi around a hundred-year-old Banyan tree, ending his Jai Alai playing career.

The Suarez-Kong operation produced millions in profits for the group that became known as the Miami Bettors' Club, but gamblers are all the same; no matter how much they win, it's never enough. Suarez figured if the Miami Bettors' Club was rolled out into all the other frontons, they'd be laying out a lot of cash for payoffs, money that would eat into their potential earnings.

In the long run, it would be cheaper to buy the league and eliminate most of the bribes. When Suarez approached Gordon's son, Freddy, with a lowball offer to purchase the operation, Gordon knew it was time to get out; but selling to Suarez was a nonstarter. As a business executive, Gordon understood Suarez's expansion plans, but he was concerned that kind of expansion would attract the attention of the FBI; and that was a nightmare Gordon didn't need. Even if he unloaded the league to Suarez, the FBI could still make an issue of his past association with a known underworld figure.

Out of the blue, Gordon received a call from William Stone, art dealer, financier, and owner of the Murphy Peanut Butter Corporation, with an inquiry regarding purchasing the league. Stone is married to Jesse James, Vice President of the Hancock Entertainment Corporation. Since the Hancock already operates racetracks with pari-mutuel betting in California, Canada, Mexico, and Argentina, they felt Jai Alai, with its pari-mutuel *raison d'être*, would be a perfect fit.

It seemed, Stone had contacts at the WSN Broadcast System that specialized in televising horse races and other international sporting events. A TV contract could be just the thing to turn Jai Alai into the next big sport's league. WSN was interested but only if Stone could find a sponsor. The whole deal hinged on Gordon agreeing to get his other major investment, InfoSilo, to sponsor the telecasts. Gordon was desperate to get out of the gambling business even if it meant barely breaking even on the sale. A deal was finally struck: Stone purchased the International Jai Alai League and Gordon got InfoSilo to sponsor the telecasts for a minimum of five years with an option for an additional three seasons. Benny Silver was sent to meet Gordon to get the television contract signed. Suarez and Kong were not happy. Kong had a history with Johnny Luck and his associates, a history that almost got him killed.

Suarez miscalculated the situation when he had Kong arrange for Gordon's murder. The situation got worse when Jesse sent her people into the Miami fronton to clean out the corruption. It was a definite setback for the Miami Bettors' Club, but that didn't deter Suarez. A new plan was put in place with a focus on the league's new showcase Jai Alai palace, the Hancock Fronton. As far as Suarez was concerned Gordon was an obstacle that had to be eliminated; all Stone did by buying the league was replace Gordon. The sale of the league to Stone was merely another obstacle that had to be eliminated.

THE GAME

4
The Game

Jai Alai literally translated means a *merry festival*.
It's been played for four hundred years in the
Basque region of Spain. Its current modern form
was developed around 1875 and is known locally
as *zesta-puta*. Originally it was played up against
a village's church wall on Sundays or during fes-
tivals. It has been described as the fastest and
most dangerous sport in the world. Proponents
and fans have dubbed it the *game of dodging
death* and *the ballet of bullets*.

The acrobatic players attempt to avoid getting hit
in the head while catching a goatskin wrapped
Brazilian rubber hardball about three-quarters
the size of a baseball. The ball or *pelota* is caught
in a wicker basket strapped to the player's right
hand. Players must catch and throw the pelota in
one continuous fluid motion at a forty-foot-high
and forty-foot-wide granite wall. The pelota has
been clocked coming off the wall at one hundred
and eighty-eight-miles an hour. Players can make
the pelota do tricks by applying various kinds of
spins using the hand-strapped basket of reeds
called a *cesta*.

The pelota can bounce ten feet into the air and
ricochet off the left-side wall forcing players to
defy gravity by athletically climbing high-up onto
the wall or fearlessly diving onto the concrete

floor in order to save a point. Players must pay careful attention and keep their eye on the pelota as the consequences of getting hit can be deadly.

Jai Alai is handball for people with a death wish. Spectators are protected by netting on the right-hand side of the open one-hundred and seventy-six foot long *cancha* or court. Despite the sport's exciting and often dangerous death-defying acrobatic performances, it is nothing more than an excuse to gamble. Jai Alai betting utilizes a pari-mutuel system that offers standard win, place, and show bets, plus trifectas, quinellas, and assorted other exotic wagers, but instead of horses, dogs, or camels, you bet on Basque athletes.

A match is a series of round-robin games involving eight singles players or eight teams of two players each. Players wear white pants often belted with a red sash called a *faja* and color-identifying t-shirts with their post ranking on the front and team number on the back. The first and second posted teams play first, with the winner moving on to play the next posted team, and the loser going to the back of the line. One point is awarded to the winner of each game in round one. Winners of second-round games earn two points. The first team to earn seven or nine points wins the match. Teams are ranked and odds are calculated much the same as they are in horse racing.

Jai Alai reached its height of popularity in the fifties and sixties in Florida where there were a number of Jai Alai frontons, although the game was also played in several other cities across the US, Mexico, and the Philippines. There is no doubt the sport is exciting for spectators and potential television audiences, but the real financial gravy lies in the revenue from pari-mutuel betting, making Jai Alai the perfect add-on gambling vehicle for the ever-expanding Hancock Entertainment Corporation.

On paper, everything made sense to Johnny Luck, but his boss, Benson Yeung, Hong Mian triad Dragon Head, had his doubts. He was an old man and he'd seen Jai Alai at its peak in the sixties. Despite its isolated, localized popularity it never reached broad market appeal and eventually, it tanked. Its recent resurgence under Walter Cummings Gordon may just be a flash-in-the-pan. Benson's concerns were real. Even the current success of the IJAL was limited to specific markets, and it depended heavily on a few hyperbolic fans and gambling junkies who bet on anything. If Luck wanted to pursue this opportunity, Benson had to be convinced. It wasn't until Luck ran his idea by his protégé, the pretty blonde ex-jockey, Jesse James, that the feasibility of investing started to make sense.

Luck: "So what do you think? Benson thinks it's crazy. I think it's a perfect supplement to the racetrack. Give those bums something to bet on when the horses aren't running."

Jesse: "What about the casino and the club? We already offer slots and all the other casino games and; there's the Shanghai Players Club for the high rollers. Benson's got a point."

Luck: "Yeah, but not everybody is comfortable in casinos, and the Shanghai is restricted to big shots. Gambler's like the action, football, baseball, even hockey. You got to give people a show. It's gladiatorial. People want blood. You ever watch the cooking channel on television, they've turned baking cookies into a blood sport. Today everything has to be a fucking contest with winners and losers, and as long as there are contests, people will want to bet on the winner. Sitting in an adult diaper pushing a button on a slot machine has its limitations. Shit... they used to call them 'one-arm-bandits' because you had to pull a lever, now all you do is press a button. People, guys particularly, want action, danger, and blood; that's why horse racing will never die, no matter how many obituaries are printed."

Jesse: "Is that what you told Benson?"

Luck: "Nah, Benson thinks like an accountant. All he wants to know is, how much will it cost, and how much can we make without going to jail?"

Jesse: "Do they really have contests for baking cookies?"

Luck: "I watched one the other day about scrabbling eggs for Christ's sake. I'm telling you, people will bet on anything."

Jesse: "You know, you may have hit on something."

Luck: "What? You want we should have a cooking contest with pari-mutuel betting?"

Jesse: "Don't be stupid, you got the solution, you just don't know it."

Luck: "You going to tell me or do I have to guess?"

Jesse: "Not only will people bet on anything, they'll watch anything, as long as it's on television, and it's promoted as some kind of contest. If they'll watch idiots scrabbling eggs, they'll watch Spanish acrobats trying to kill one another with a rubber ball. You get this shit on television and you'll get international market penetration. You said it yourself, gamblers want action, excitement, and danger, Give them a televised blood sport with winners and losers and people will bet. You get this cockamamie sport on the tube and not only will you fill the stands, you'll have massive OTB."

Luck: "You right. Maybe we could talk to some-one at one of the broadcast networks. Doesn't Stone play squash with that guy from WSN, Benny something."

Jesse: "Benny Silver"

Luck: "Run this by Stone and have him contact Silver. Have Stone tell Silver, he's interested in purchasing the IJAL but only if he can get a tele-vision contract."

William Stone is Jesse's husband and a friend of the Hong Mian. The ex-British MI6 spook is a fi-nancial genius, a former stock market manipula-tor, and the man responsible for laundering the proceeds of the Hong Mian's various illegal oper-ations. He is also responsible for the distribution of Hong Mian's cocaine throughout the United States through his multimillion-dollar corpora-tion, the Murphy Peanut Butter Company.

Jesse: "What's in it for Silver?

Luck: "We'll make him President of the League. If he can convince the network to put Jai Alai on television, I think Benson will okay the deal."

Two weeks later Benny Silver finds himself in the hundred and ten degree Spicebush Fundamental-ist Church listening to an obese demagogue, equating belief in God to buying milk.

A month later, the construction of the Hancock Jai Alai Fronton is started. The sports' pages of the LA Times are filled with pictures and stories of Benjamin Silver, the new President of the re-structured International Jai Alai League with frontons in Miami, Atlantic City, Las Vegas, Reno, and the new LA, Hancock Jai Alai stadium. Future plans include adding frontons in Crystal Beach, Ontario and Tijuana, Mexico, with both sites conveniently located near the US border.

THE CLUB

5
The Club

The murder of William Cummings Gordon made the national newspapers; his position as Chairman of InfoSilo, a major government subcontractor associated with various intelligence agencies made for interesting speculation, not to mention, any number of wild conspiracy theories involving foreign governments of which Benjamin Silver was rumored to be an agent.

Silver was questioned as to why he was with Gordon at the Spicebush Golf Club and why he made such a hasty getaway. As much as the local police would have liked to pin the whole thing on Silver, there just wasn't any evidence that he was involved. Eventually, the murder was blamed on an illegal immigrant who managed to get a job as a gardener at the club. No one questioned why some poor working stiff would kill Gordon; the fact that he was an illegal immigrant was enough to satisfy the locals of his guilt. Although the gardener escaped the scene of the crime, the police eventually tracked him down three days later, only to find his body in a dumpster behind the Spicebush Garden Center.

The truth is Gordon was killed because his son Freddy couldn't convince his father to sell the IJAL to Peruvian gangster, Marco Antonio Suarez, *El Astronauta*, the man who ran a gambling syndicate that had infiltrated the IJAL. Suarez, like Freddy, was not aware that Gordon already sold the league to Stone. Suarez assumed, with the senior Gordon out of the way, Freddy would inherit the league giving him and his associate Tommy Kong complete operational control from the inside. The fact that Freddy was wounded by a stray bullet was merely an accident. Unlike the movies, murders are rarely without collateral damage.

Suarez's Jai Alai gambling operation is known as the Miami Bettor's Club. It's based out of the Miami fronton. Suarez's partner, Tommy Kong, uses player intimidation and pay-offs to league officials in order to gain an advantage. The corrupt fronton employees supply club members with time-sensitive pari-mutuel statistics that in combination with fixed matches provide the club with maximum payouts that are just under the limit for IRS scrutiny.

If Freddy would have become President of the league, the Miami Bettor's Club would have been able to control the wagering in all the frontons. The murder of Freddy's old man was a miscalculation. In order to cut their losses and put an end to any further police investigation, the imported South American gardener-hitman had to be eliminated. Even without the insider control, Suarez figured he could buy the influence he needed to expand the club into all the league's locations.

The question now was simple: how would the Hong Mian react to the Miami Bettor's Club expanding into the other locations, including the newly built Hancock fronton?

Tommy Kong already had a history with the Hong Mian and he hadn't forgotten how they blew-up the Jiangshi Motorcycle Clubhouse, killing most of his fellow gang members. He only survived the blast because he was sitting on the toilet in the back of the club. The fire investigators found him in the can with his pants down, half dead, that's not something you easily forget.

MATTIE HENRY

6
Mattie Henry

The lobby buzzer startled Mattie despite the fact she expected a visitor. She stared down at the white porcelain bowl filled with sugar cubes.

She placed the syringe back into its leather pouch. She tightened the cap on the bottle of Xylazine. She placed the leather pouch, the sugar cubes, and the bottle in the cupboard under the island stovetop.

Mattie had been living in the condo for three years, but she rarely spent any time in the kitchen. Mattie Henry wasn't much of a cook. Homemaking, in general, is something women like Mattie regard as the reserve of grandmothers and homely unfortunates, and Mattie definitely did not fall into either category.

Mattie is one of those women that find themselves lost in a purgatorial demographic, too old to be a snowflake Millennial and too young to be a condescending Gen Xer; a female constituency that feels any time spent in the kitchen is akin to a life sentence on a Maricopa County chain gang.

The necessity of sustenance is something to be provided or purchased, not something that you make yourself. Domestic drudgery is for others, not Mattie Henry. It is not that Mattie is concerned about getting her hands dirty, at least not in the metaphorical sense. Dipping her hands in a bowl of flour and eggs seems somehow demeaning, but the stench of psychological and political gamesmanship smells like victory to people like Mattie. For her, the aroma of winning is more intoxicating than the smell of freshly baked bread. Women like Mattie with movie star good looks and national television exposure rarely eat alone, almost never pay, and seldom find themselves in need of a frying pan.

Mattie Henry is the most visible female presence on the WSN Sport's Network, but despite her high profile and hefty salary, she assumes she is being shafted; the seed of discontent fostered and encouraged in the radical corners of the feminist cabal. Mattie expected to be handed the eleven o'clock co-anchor position, the most prestigious job in sport's television broadcasting, but the board of WSN felt she wasn't ready. She tried everything to convince them, including sabotaging her rivals' on-air interviews and fucking half the members of the executive search committee. It didn't work, despite her carnal expertise; a competency that got her expelled from one of the country's top equine veterinary universities for simultaneously sleeping with three of her married professors.

From failed horse doctor to broadcasting sexpot, was not as big a leap as one might imagine. Women with dazzling looks and rapacious predatory sexual natures easily slither into self-aggrandizing positions, but sometimes even a practiced Mata Hari ends up facing a firing squad.

Instead of getting the top anchor post, Mattie was given the horse racing assignment. She was reduced to traveling the country, interviewing jockeys, owners, and trainers anytime there was a broadcast-worthy stake race. Initially, she resented the expulsion from network Primetime, but Mattie knew her looks and aggressive self-promoting would eventually get her released from the gulag of secondary sports' broadcasting. It was only a matter of time; besides the horse racing gig had its advantages. Getting to know the trainers, vets, and jockeys led to a significant amount of insider information, especially from the horny little horsemen that were willing to spill their guts for a chance to get up close and personal with the lovely television personality.

It is important for the racetracks to maintain good relations with the media and as such Mattie was given free rein to wander around shed row whenever she wanted. Around the backstretch, Mattie is called *Sugar* for her practice of feeding the horses sugar cubes that she always carried in her WSN media-jacket pocket. It's assumed the treats are a way of ingratiating the pretty reporter to her high-strung equine subjects, which in part is true, but occasionally when the odds are just right, the benign sugar treats become Xylazine dosed sedatives, just strong enough to turn a sure winner into an also-ran. Mattie's time in veterinarian school wasn't wasted.

The condo buzzer sounds again. Mattie looks at her Tag Heuer. Benny Silver is right on time. She knows Benny from his time at WSN and she knows he's just been appointed President of the IJAL. Maybe this is her ticket out of the horse shit and back onto Primetime. Mattie presses the button to open the lobby entrance allowing Silver into the building. A few minutes later there's a knock. Mattie opens the door. Standing in the hallway is Benny Silver, the newly appointed President of the IJAL, Jesse James, the Director of the Hancock Racetrack, and a handsome forty-something Spaniard she didn't know. Benny is an old colleague, he greets Mattie with a perfunctory kiss on the cheek.

Benny: "Hope you don't mind, I brought a couple of colleagues to our little get-together?"

Mattie: "Sure, no problem, I've been trying to get an interview with Miss James for some time. She's got quite the reputation in the racing and casino world."

Jesse: "I'm not the publicity seeking type."

Mattie: "You didn't mind when you raced."

Jesse: "That was then, this is now. I'm just a cog in the wheel like everyone else."

Mattie: "That's not what I hear. People say you're Johnny Luck's go-to girl. You got your fingers in all the sticky pots." Before Jesse can answer Benny interrupts. He motions toward the handsome Spaniard, "This is Xavier Gebara."

Gebara takes Mattie's hand and kisses it. Mattie smiles, "Mr. Gebara is quite the Latin charmer."

Gebara bows, "*Nire atsegina*."

Mattie: "That doesn't sound Spanish?"

Gebara: "It's Basque."

Mattie: "Well then, you're either a separatist or a Jai Alai player."

Gebara: "A good guess, dear lady. I am an ex-Jai Alai player. Quite a good one in my day if you don't mind me saying."

Mattie looks him over like he's the second coming of Magic Mike, "You look like you could still score a few points."

Benny: "Xavier was in a car accident last year. He had a pretty bad concussion. The doctors won't okay him to play anymore."

Mattie: "Too bad, I'd have liked to seen him play."

Jesse: "Which is sort of why we're here."

Mattie: "I'm all ears."

Mattie heard the scuttlebutt surrounding the murder of Walter Cummings Gordon and the takeover of the International Jai Alai League by financier William Stone, Jesse's husband. It's common knowledge in the circles that count that Jesse James is a triad asset, a racetrack, casino and gambling executive, and Johnny Luck's protégé. Her relationship with Stone in and of itself is enough to cause speculation. Rumors about Stone have been floating around for years, ever since he inherited the Murphy Peanut Butter Corporation from his employer who died in a tragic car accident in Palermo, Sicily. Speculation abounded about why Murphy would leave the bulk of her billion dollar estate to her English chauffeur, but then stranger things have been done by the eccentric rich.

Why a Hong Kong big swinging dick financial boffin like Stone would take a job as a rich lady's chauffeur and personal assistant was another question that was never answered. When news media investigators dug into Stone's background they found they hit a dead end. He seemed to appear magically out of nowhere. Reporters were warned to stay clear, and if they persisted, they found a pink-slip clipped to their final paycheck. The digging stopped, but not the rumors.

Mattie understood if Jesse James and William Stone were involved in this deal, there was big money on the line, and she wanted in. Mattie wouldn't be disappointed. She is offered the job to co-host the Primetime International Jai Alai Broadcasts on the WSN television network with ex-Jai Alai champion, Xavier Javier Diego Gebara.

BO TANG

7
Bo Tang

The WSN Sports Network initially envisioned Jai Alai as a tertiary time-filler like poker, something to fill dead time slots until something better came along. They assumed the reconfigured Jai Alai league would go the way of 'Slamball' and similar televised athletic gimmicks like women's lingerie football. What the WSN executives didn't understand is getting in bed with William Stone and associates is a lifetime commitment, an obligation that is more likely to result in their personal termination rather than the cancellation of the Jai Alai broadcasts.

The extent of the WSN commitment was made clear when Stone and Jesse paid a visit to the President of the network who obviously didn't get the message. He made it clear he regarded Stone as a dilettante and Jesse as a lightweight television wannabe. He heard the rumors of Jesse's involvement with the Chinese, but he figured he was too high-profile to be a serious target. His opinion changed before he left the parking garage on his way home that evening. His Mercedes wouldn't start. When he opened the hood to find out what the problem was, he found a note that simply read "BOOM!" Just in case he couldn't figure out who the note was from, the message was repeated underneath in Chinese.

The President of WSN wouldn't be canceling the Jai Alai broadcasts anytime soon.

Shortly after the car trouble, the President of WSN announced that in addition to the Jai Alai broadcasts, a weekly Primetime television show hosted by Mattie Henry and Xavier Gebara featuring interviews, profiles, and highlights from all the frontons across the country would be instituted. Mattie in what became her signature sexy wardrobe interviewed the star players and guest celebrity fans; Gebara explained the finer points of the game and handicapped the teams for novice punters looking to participate in what became the hottest game in town. Johnny and Jesse made sure movie and music celebrities, especially those that carried a deficit balance at the Hancock, kept the news media busy covering the new gambling venture. Even the President of WSN became an enthusiastic booster, as soon as he saw the television audience numbers skyrocket. Fans held weekly Jai Alai parties and inquiries about new franchises poured in from big city mayors across the country. The opening of the Hancock Fronton became a major LA event. Sports' celebrities, movie stars, and politicians like Governor Somersby arrived on the red carpet to be interviewed by Mattie Henry and her TV partner Xavier Gebara.

Fans flocked to all the existing frontons around the country with the Hancock the place to go to see movie stars, watch Jai Alai, and most importantly, lose money. Food was another aspect of the Hancock that attracted high-end customers. The Hancock Fronton featured one of the best Chinese restaurants in the city. The dining room overlooked the *cancha* or court, so customers could dine in comfort while watching the matches. The menu included rare Chinese delicacies created by the expert chefs from the Green Dragon Restaurant, the headquarters of Benson Yeung, Hong Mian Dragon Head, and Johnny Luck's boss. The dining room incorporated several private boxes reserved for big shots and corporate clients eager to show their customers a good time. Waiters and waitresses didn't just take food orders, they took bets as well; gamblers never had to leave their seats.

Anytime a business, legitimate or otherwise, has success, predatory opportunists will want to take a piece of the pie, and in the case of the Hancock Fronton, those ravenous pie eaters are Antonio Suarez and Tommy Kong. Although Suarez only made occasional appearances, Kong and a group of MBC associates became nightly fixtures in one of the private boxes. The waiter in charge of that private dining room is Bo Tang. He takes their bets and orders their food. They over-tip Tang and treat him as if he's part of the crew. Tang likes the attention and the big tips even more.

Kong waves for Tang to come over. He is surrounded by associates who are all sitting waiting for the next match to start. Kong takes a large roll

of bills out of this pocket. He hands Tang cash
and a betting slip with a Quinella Wheel wager
featuring Team Three: as long as Team Three is
either first or second in combination with any of
the other seven teams, he wins. Kong reaches up
with one very large hand and takes Tang by the
collar. He pulls Tang's head down close enough to
his face that Tang's chin is tickled by the
whiskers of Kong's massive white Fu Manchu. He
slips a hundred dollar bill into Tang's black Hancock uniform shirt pocket. "There's a lot more
where that came from if you're interested. Meet
me at the State Diner, tomorrow at eleven. I'll buy
you breakfast. I hear they got pretty good
muffins." Kong releases his grip. Tang returns to
his usual position by the door.

The next morning at eleven AM sharp, Tang
walks through the door of the long riveted silver-
tube known as the State Diner operated by Carman and her foul-mouth Chinese short-order
cook husband, Barney. Sitting at the counter is
Mattie Henry enjoying one of Barney's gigantic
blueberry muffins and a coffee. Mattie couldn't
help but notice the oversized bald Chinese ape
sitting a few tables in front of a guy who appeared to be asleep in the back table under a
convex mirror. She's seen the Chinese Goliath
around; he was hard to miss. She couldn't remember if it was at the track or the fronton. One
look and Mattie knew the tattooed behemoth is
no civilian; it really isn't a surprise since the
Hancock complex is crawling with Chinese char-

acters in all shapes and sizes. She didn't give the guy a second thought until the front aluminum door rattled open and the image of Bo Tang appeared in the shiny metal surface of the old fashion napkin dispenser. She recognized Bo from the Hancock Fronton. Mattie makes it her business to know every face that works at the stadium and the track. You never know when someone might become useful. She rarely had to do much to convince male colleagues to play along with whatever she had in mind.

Mattie lingers longer than necessary nursing her third cup of coffee. She repositions the reflective napkin dispenser so it gives her a perfect view of Bo Tang and his new pal, Tommy The King Kong. Carman and Barney watch with practiced interest. Barney takes out his mobile phone and surreptitiously takes a picture of Kong and Tang. He then casually focuses on Mattie. She's too engrossed in the image in the napkin dispenser to notice.

Like Mattie, Carman made it her business to know everybody that is anybody at the Hancock. It isn't that she's nosey, it's part of her business, Hong Mian business. If you looked closely, you'd notice Barney wore a Guan Yu pin signifying his full membership in LA's most powerful triad. As Tommy Kong got up to leave, he put a thick paw on Bo Tang's shoulder forcing him back down into his seat. Mattie watches the scene play out in the reflection of the napkin dispenser. Bo waits another five minutes, looks at his Timex, gets up and leaves. Mattie looks up from the napkin dispenser to see Carman has been eyeballing her the entire time.

Carman: "Women used to carry compacts in their purses for that trick, but I guess with your looks, makeup is redundant." Mattie smiles, making an attempt to appear innocent, but innocent is not in Mattie's repertoire, besides, as far as Carman is concerned, nobody is innocent.

Mattie: "Who's the oversized Jeff to the skinny Mutt?"

Carman can't help but smile. "Kind of an old reference for such a young thing."

Mattie: "Well I guess I'm just an old fashion girl at heart, besides, I did some voice-over for a documentary on the early comic strips."

Carman: "*The Funny Paper Chronicles*, yeah, I saw it on The Learning Channel. My husband didn't get it." Barney leans over the open counter from the kitchen and says something in Cantonese. Carman responds in kind.

Mattie: "You speak Chinese?" It's more of a statement than a question.

Carman: "Better than my husband speaks English."

Mattie figures she's made a friend with the chitchat: "So do you know the big guy? Does he come in often?"

Carman: "Can't really say. We have a lot of customers. People all start to look alike after a while. They like the muffins, especially the chocolate chip."

Mattie takes a ten dollar bill and places it on the counter. "You get a lot of three-hundred pound, bald, tattooed Chinese gangsters, with white Fu Manchu moustaches that weigh more than I do?"

Carman: "You'd be surprised who we get in here Hun." Carman pockets the ten spot not bothering to offer change. Mattie smiles, she gets the message. "You come back soon Hun, I'll save you one of Barney's chocolate muffins, they're to die for."

Mattie takes notice of Carman's name tag pinned to her white shirt; she takes a card out of her purse along with a twenty dollar bill. She places both on the counter. "Do me favor Carman, either Mutt or Jeff come back, give me a call."

Carman slips the twenty into her apron pocket. She picks up the card and looks at it. "Thought you looked familiar, you do the Jai Ali broadcasts."

Mattie reaches for the front door. "Those two come back, call me. There's another twenty and free dinner tickets to the Jai Alai if they do. Your husband looks like the kind of man that likes to place the occasional wager." She leaves. Barney says something rude in Cantonese. Carman responds, "*Biǎo zi!*" She takes the mobile phone out of her apron pocket and dials a number. Jesse answers.

Carman: "How ya do'in Hun? It's Carman.

Jesse: "Hi Carman, you going to save me a chocolate for breakfast."

Carman: "Don't I always? Listen Hun... I might have something that will interest you. Tommy Kong was in here meeting some skinny dude and they weren't making plans for Chinese New Year."

Jesse: "Yeah, Kong and Suarez are trying to horn-in on the Jai Alai operation. Their cronies are at the matches every night. You recognize the other guy?"

Carman: "Nah, but Barney took a picture with his phone."

Jesse: "Has he learned how to focus it yet?"

Carman: "Yeah, I had him taking pictures of Arlo sleeping in the corner. I figure he never moves, so it's good practice. Something else... that tootsie who does the Jai Alai broadcasts was in here at the same time. She seemed really interested in Tommy. Wanted to know if I knew who he was. She must have known the skinny guy cause she didn't ask about him."

Jesse: "I just got Barney's pictures. You're right the woman is Mattie Henry, she does the Jai Alai broadcasts with Xavier Gebara. Tell Barney he gets a big kiss when I come for breakfast but next time tell him to focus on the eyes, not the tits."

Carman: "Should I call her if Kong and the other guy comes back?"

Jesse: "Call me first. See if you can eavesdrop and get a sense of what they're discussing. I think the other guy works in the dining room at the fronton. It looks like Kong and Suarez are trying to pull the same scheme they had going in Miami when Gordon ran the League. They weren't happy when we shut them down. It sounds like they want to resurrect the scam at the Hancock. These guys got balls. It's a good thing they don't have the brains to match, but why Mattie Henry would be interested, is something else."

SOLO AND MENDOZA

8
Solo and Mendoza

Jai Alai like tennis can be played as either a singles' or doubles' match. The Hancock Fronton features doubles matches on Tuesday, Thursday, and Saturday and singles matches on Monday, Wednesday, and Friday. The top singles' player in the league is Bolivar Solo, a handsome Basque star with a reputation amongst the ladies that would rival Wilt Chamberlain who claimed to have bedded twenty thousand women; a mathematical improbability since he died at the tender age of sixty-three, a not surprising premature end if his claim was anything close to accurate.

Bolivar is the poster boy for the league, extremely good-looking, exotically foreign, and athletically expert. When he plays, the fans shout "*¡Mucho Solo!*" He is exactly what the league needs to sell Jai Alai to the American public: a fan base that demands celebrity superstardom as much as skilled athleticism. His doubles' partner and protégé is the up-and-coming star Gorka Mendoza. When these two superstars enter a nightclub, cell phones explode in a burst of spontaneous admiration, each wanting to capture evidence that they were there when...

On this particular evening, Solo and Mendoza choose the Oasis Club as the place to go to blow off steam and exercise their excess sexual energy.

They sit drinking Dom Perignon in a private entertainment room surrounded by the four loveliest ladies in the club. Mendoza stands, pulling one of the women up off the red leather circular couch. He wants to dance to the Latin beat being played by the DJ. Solo and the other women laugh as Mendoza twirls his willing partner around like a top until she unsteadily falls into the arms of Tommy The King Kong who is standing in the doorway beside Marco Antonio Suarez.

Suarez: *"Buenas noches mis amigos."*

Kong unleashes the young woman from his grip and pushes her back onto the red couch with more force than is necessary or appreciated. "We need to talk." Solo looks at Mendoza who shrugs his shoulders. Neither Bolivar nor Gorka knows who these two characters are but they've been around long enough to recognize the signs.

Suarez: "I believe now is a convenient time."

Kong: "Get rid of the broads." Solo tells the women to go to the bar and wait for them. The women reluctantly leave each giving Kong and Suarez nasty looks for spoiling their fun. Kong drops his massive bulk down on the red couch beside Mendoza, forcing the air in the cushions along the settee, almost propelling Solo onto the floor. Kong pours himself a glass of Champagne.

Suarez: "We're here to discuss a business opportunity."

Solo: "I'm afraid you have to discuss that with our agent. He looks after all that kind of thing. We just play Jai Alai."

Suarez: "It's not that kind of business deal. It's the kind you wouldn't want your agent or anybody else to know about."

Solo: "No offense, but you got the wrong guys. We don't do that."

Kong takes a giant swig of Dom Perignon draining the glass. He fills the empty goblet with what's left in the Champagne bottle. "Oh, you're the right guys alright. You're the exact guys we need."

Suarez: "What do you know about Ola and Urbina?"

Mendoza: "They're competitors... rookies."

Solo: "They're talented but inexperienced. They haven't learned how to win yet."

Suarez: "In other words, the odds on them coming in first this Thursday will be high?"

Mendoza: "Sure. There are too many good teams ahead of them. They'll be posted eighth, guaranteed, and eight almost never wins."

Kong: "Perfect! That makes for a nice Exacta wheel with them on the front end."

Suarez: "You're going to play Ola and Urbina and you're going to lose."

Solo: "First of all, no one will believe we legitimately lost to those '*novatos*'; and more to the point, we won't do it."

Suarez: "You let us worry about what people believe, and as far as your moral qualms are concerned, I don't think you want the LA newspapers to find out about that incident in Miami a few years back. It seems a West Palm motel manager made a lot of money on a match you lost to Mattin Zabala, a guy you previously beat six times in a row. Something about an eighteen-year-old freshman that OD'd in your hotel room. You should never pay for a room with a credit card; always pay cash, you never know when some bitch will overindulge."

Solo: "That loss was legit; I was injured. It had nothing to do with that woman's overdose. She's fine. I hear she's running for town council."

Suarez: "Whatever you say. You're going to lose or you're going to get hurt for real. It's as simple as that. If necessary fake an injury, have a heart attack, I really don't give a shit how you lose, just lose! Everything has been arranged. Do your part, and everyone goes home happy and richer."

Solo: "You can make as many arrangements as you want, but not with us. We don't throw matches."

Kong: "Oh you'll throw this one or they'll be consequences."

Suarez reaches into his jacket pocket and takes out a thick manila envelope. He tosses it on the table in front of Solo and his partner. The edges of several one-hundred-dollar bills slip out the open side. Mendoza lifts the edge of the envelope with one finger. It's at least five thousand dollars.

JA CUBIERTO! - DUCK!

9
¡a cubierto!
Duck!

Friday evening Mattie Henry and Xavier Gebara enter the communication's center where reporters watch the matches and write their stories. Mattie and Gebara glad-hand their way through the room kibitzing with the sports' writers on their way to the adjacent media room. The state-of-the-art broadcast booth is located just under the dining room and private boxes and over the general admission booths. Each general admission cubicle is equipped with a touch screen tablet so customers can place bets and review highlights. Attractive usherettes go up and down the isles taking food orders and collecting money.

Mattie and Gebara settle into their seats behind their microphones and replay monitors. They put on their headphones as the pulse-pounding Latin House theme plays over spectacular video highlights of *pelotaris* climbing the side wall or diving to the floor in order to return a shot. Gebara and Mattie swivel their chairs around to face the camera and introduce the evenings matches featuring the top team in the country, Solo and Mendoza.

Tonight, Kong and Suarez preside over their group of MBC gambling associates in their usual private dining room. Suarez normally stays away from the fronton leaving Kong to be the point man for the Jai Alai operation, but tonight is different. This is the night Solo and Mendoza are supposed to tank their prearranged match with Ola and Urbina. If everyone plays their part, it means the MBC group has successfully corrupted all the players on the Hancock roster, but that is only half of their plan. In order to maximize profits, they also need inside information on how much money and how many people are betting on each team. To avoid detection, the group has to be selective. They can't fix every match, that would make it too easy for Jesse and her Hong Mian overseers to trace the scam back to Suarez and Kong who are already on their radar. Instead, they need to pick matches where the return is substantial but still under the IRS's threshold for withholding twenty percent.

The problem is, Jai Alai is a round robin format. You never know what the actual individual matches will be unless you pay off all sixteen pelotaris on the roster. You could get away with corrupting just one player on each team but that could ultimately backfire if someone's partner got their nose out of joint. The smartest thing to do is pay everyone. With every pelotari corrupted, Kong and Suarez will be able to fix any match they want. What's needed now is inside information on how much money and how many people are betting on each team or player on a minute by minute basis which brings us to Terrance

Lebow, the Pari-Mutuel Manager. For the scheme to work Terrance or Terry as he likes to be called, has to be corrupted. Suarez and Kong know, or at least assume, that everyone has skeletons hidden in their closet. Sometimes you have to look hard like in the case of the relatively clean Bolivar Solo, but dig a little deeper and dirt will eventually turn-up. Money may be the leading incentive for inducing moral decay, but blackmail and threats of physical violence can also serve as effective inducements. Combine the three in a trifecta of ethical ambivalence like in the case of Bolivar Solo and you're sure to have a convincing incentive.

In the case of Terrance, Terry Lebow, dressing up in women's clothes and carousing with like-minded nonconformists at The Molly House made blackmail the most obvious corruptor du jour. It is, of course, sweetened with threats of physical harm, topped-off with a little cash, just to make sure Terry's conscious didn't succumb to spiralling self-loathing and indignant moral outrage.

Suarez and Kong had all the pieces in place to guarantee a continual hefty return on their investment. Now all they needed was Solo and Mendoza to play ball. The evening's matches went as planned. Everyone played their part; the pelotaris all did what they were paid to do and Lebow emailed pari-mutuel statistics to Tang who then passed them on to Kong every ninety seconds. If they could successfully pull-off the evening's ruse, it would be a major accomplishment considering the number of moving parts involved. There is only one hurdle left to overcome, the match between Solo-Mendoza and Ola-Urbina. All the evening's winnings were riding on the Exacta placing Ola-Urbina first and Solo-Mendoza second: they had to finish in that exact order for the bet to pay off. Since Ola-Urbina were posted eighth, the numbers were very attractive.

A Jai Ali cancha or court is divided into fourteen sections with lines designating each division. The server must bounce the ball once behind the serving line, line eleven, catch it in his *cesta* and fire it at the front granite wall so it lands somewhere between line four and seven. The match-game begins with Solo serving. He expertly lands the pelota just over the designated service landing line forcing Ola to dive, roll, and return a hard but defensive reply. The pelota comes off the wall low and fast but Mendoza, playing in the front court has no problem directing it so it comes off the granite heading for the side wall.

Ola attempts to catch the carom high off the side wall but the pelota hits the wall just out of his reach. The pelota hits the floor with an awkward spin pushing it towards the out-of-bounds area bordered by the protective audience screen. Urbina races from his backcourt position catching the hard goatskin covered projectile before it hits the screen returning it before it gives Solo and Mendoza the winning point.

Urbina's shot comes off the front surface high and long, looping over everyone's head. Solo races back hoping the pelota doesn't hit low on the back wall for an impossible-to-return kill-shot. He picks the goatskin out of mid-air as he acrobatically climbs the back wall, simultaneously somersaulting and twisting like an Olympic diver. In one fluid motion, he flings the pelota toward the front granite surface. The fans are on their feet screaming "*¡Mucho Solo! ¡Mucho Solo! ¡Mucho Solo!*"

Urbina is out of position from the previous shot but Ola races to the backcourt catching the goatskin as it comes down. He slides, rolls, and twists to his feet with a desperate sidearm return to save the point, but the return has little force. Everyone holds their breath as the pelota lazily sails towards the front wall. In the MBC private box, Kong and Suarez push their colleagues out of the way in order to get a better look.

Solo yells "*¡Libra!, ¡Libra!*" signaling Mendoza to race towards the front wall. Mendoza dives to the cancha floor catching the pelota in his cesta just before it hits the court and in a single motion rolls, fires, and bounces to his feet. The pelota comes off the granite heading towards the side-wall, but Urbina sees it. He climbs the wall making an excellent save. The return heads for the out-of-bounds area. It lands just in fair territory, but Solo is experienced enough to gauge the pelota's trajectory. He catches the ball in foul territory before it hits the screen and fires it towards the front corner.

Ola hollers "*¡Carombola!*" warning Urbina that Solo's shot will carom off the front wall and hit the sidewall in a manner that will be almost impossible to return. Ola races towards the front court to help. The pelota comes off the sidewall in a severe angle with an acute spin. It hits the cancha floor just out of Urbina's reach. He stretches out to catch it, but he's underestimated the angle and spin. He misses it entirely. The pelota heads for the spectator-protective screen. Ola races forward leaving his feet in a futile attempt to save the game but he comes up short. He slides across the cancha floor as the pelota bounces off the screen and dribbles harmlessly down the length of the court. The referee signals "*Tanto* Solo-Mendoza, Game Solo-Mendoza." The fans are on their feet chanting, "Bolivar! Gorka! Bolivar! Gorka!"

In the MBC private box, Suarez and Kong are furious. Kong crushes the half-filled glass of whisky he holds in his hand. He ignores the resulting blood mixed with Chivas as it drips onto the carpeted floor. There will be consequences.

The following evening there's a singles match between Urbina and Mendoza. There's a large flat screen monitor installed in the *Palco de pelotaris* so the players can view the matches. Solo silently critiques his doubles partner's game as he gulps an energy drink from a plastic bottle supplied by the fronton. He feared there would be retribution. He assumed they'd come after him, but he was ready. Solo takes another drink from the plastic bottle as he watches. Urbina takes a rather easy shot off the front wall, swivels, and whirls around firing his return directly at Mendoza's head. Mendoza turns just in time to avoid what could have been a real-life kill shot, but not in time to avoid it altogether. Solo helplessly barks at the monitor, "*¡a cubierto!* Duck!"

Mendoza is hit in the shoulder. He falls to the cancha floor like he was shot by .357 Magnum. Solo crushes the still half full plastic water bottle in his hand. Mendoza will be out of action for weeks. Bolivar Solo gets the message. If he doesn't do what he's told, next time, it will be him, and maybe he won't be as lucky as his partner. Punishing Solo by injuring Mendoza made sense. Solo is the big star and a perpetual favorite. Kong and Suarez want him to play.

During a commercial in the broadcast booth, Mattie Henry turns to Xavier Gebara, "Jesus, a few inches to the left and it could have killed him."

Gebara: "That was no accident." Mattie looks at her broadcast partner in disbelief.

Gebara: "That was a message!" The following week Solo does as he is told and comes up short in a singles match against Ola, who is posted eighth at big odds. Suarez and Kong make a killing of a financial kind. During a commercial after Solo loses his match, Mattie turns to Gebara, "Solo didn't look like himself tonight. You think he's injured?"

Gebara: "What did I tell you last week? The only thing wrong with Bolivar Solo is a bad case of Suarez-Kong-itis."

STILL NO CHOCOLATE

10
Still No Chocolate

Mattie Henry sits at the State Diner counter enjoying her coffee and one of Carman's butterscotch muffins; as usual, she ordered chocolate but as usual the chocolate is sold out. Mattie, like a lot of Hancock people, is a regular at the diner. Every morning she orders a chocolate muffin and coffee, and every morning the muffin is anything but chocolate, Mattie started to doubt whether Carman ever made chocolate muffins. She's positive Carman just likes to fuck with people.

Mattie closes the Daily Racing form she's been reading. Carman smiles as she watches Mattie maneuver the shiny silver napkin holder into position as the front screen door rattles open.

Tommy Kong choreographically navigates his massive frame through the not quite large enough opening; an entrance big enough for normal sized humans, but straining to accommodate Kong's king-size bulk. Kong takes a seat near the back close to where Carman's cousin, Arlo, is permanently stationed in a semi comatose posture. Mattie picks up the racing form, her coffee and muffin, swivels off her stool, and Marilyn Monroe's her way to Kong's table.

Mattie: "Mind some company?"

Kong looks Mattie over, adjusting his initial thinking, "You're not a working girl, and you're not a cop. Who are you?"

Mattie doesn't wait for a reply she takes a seat opposite Kong: "I'm Mattie Henry, I do the Jai Alai broadcasts with Xavier Gebara,"

Kong: "Sure, sure... I knew you looked familiar. No offense with the working girl crack."

Mattie: "None taken."

Carman comes to the table and drops a large black coffee and giant butterscotch muffin in front of Kong.

Kong: "What, no chocolate again?"

Carman: "I keep telling you people, you want chocolate, you got to get here early." Carman gives Mattie a wink and walks back behind the counter.

Kong: "You used to do the horse races, I remember seeing you on television. You gave a whole new meaning to the term boob-tube."

Mattie: "Thanks... I think. And I still do the horse races which is what I want to talk to you about."

Kong: "I'm listening."

Mattie: "Ever heard of *Can't Dance Don't Ask Me*?"

Kong: "Sure I like old movies, Fred Astaire and Ginger Rogers, you should watch it in Chinese. It makes no fucking sense at all."

Mattie: "It's a horse. He's running in tomorrow's Magnum Stakes." Mattie shoves the racing form across the table so Kong can see it. She's circled *Can't Dance Don't Ask Me*. Kong looks down at the form.

Kong: "Says here your nag's a dog."

Mattie: "Makes for pretty good odds, don't you think?"

Kong: "Big odds are great, if the nag's got a chance to win. This crow-bait should be pulling a milk cart. It's completely outclassed."

Mattie: "You're right. It will probably go off at close to twenty-to-one. So if I was you, I'd put a thousand on the nose."

Kong: "Sure thing, sweetheart. I'm Chinese, not stupid. If I want to blow a grand, I can think of better ways to do it."

Mattie: "Let me put it to you another way. When you think of *Can't Dance*, think of Iker Ola. The thing about horses is, you don't need threats when you got Xylazine. I do you a track favor, you do me a cancha favor. Just like Fred and Ginger, let's dance; we could make beautiful music if we work together." She reaches across the table and taps the racing form twice with her elegant index finger. "You put a thousand on that horse, then come see me." She gets up and starts to walk away.

Kong calls after her. "You forgot your racing form."

Mattie turns. "Keep it. You can pin it on the wall as a reminder of coulda, woulda, shoulda."

Kong finishes his coffee and muffin. He picks up Mattie's racing form and heads for the door. He drops the form in the trash receptacle next to the entrance. Carman waits until she hears his car drive off. She retrieves the racing form from the bin. She looks at it; it's open to the eighth race, The Magnum Stakes, number five is circled, *Can't Dance Don't Ask Me*. Carman takes her cell phone out of her apron pocket. She presses a number. "Jesse it's Carman, you've got *tsuris*."

MAKING A LIST AND CHECKING IT TWICE

11
Making A List and Checking It Twice

While Tommy Kong and his pal Antonio Suarez spend a nice relaxing Saturday afternoon at the racetrack waiting for the eighth race with the hot tip from the even hotter Mattie Henry, Bo Tang sits in his nondescript apartment kitchen hunched over his laptop analyzing the betting patterns of the MBC gamblers. There's a knock on the front door. Tang gets up and walks to the front of the apartment. He peers through the peep-hole. Terry Lebow smiles back. Five minutes later they are sitting at the kitchen table discussing how they can take advantage of their involvement with Kong and Suarez.

Lebow: "I really don't understand why you keep crunching the numbers?"

Tang: "I'm trying to figure out their system so we can piggyback our bets on top of theirs."

Lebow: "Why bother? The matches are fixed for Christ's sake, the stats are only to make sure they stay under the IRS radar. You're the one that processes the bets. That's all the information we need."

Tang: "I just thought that..."

Lebow: "Look, let me do the thinking. Who we bet on is a given. What we need to figure out is who's going to place the bets?"

Tang: "I can't do it. Management would smell a rat. Can you do it."

Lebow: "Are you crazy? I'm as vulnerable as you. We need a partner."

Tang: "Shit! Another partner, this is getting complicated."

Lebow: "We need somebody who can insulate us from scrutiny and maybe bankroll the whole operation. The only way the risk is worth it, is if we can place a lot of bets. I'm assuming you're not in any better a financial situation than I am, unless you got a lot of extra cash lying around."

Tang shakes his head. "So who do we get?"

Lebow and Tang start making a list of potential candidates. As each name is added to the list, others are crossed off. Finding the right partner seems to be a major stumbling block. Frustrated, they sink back on the cheap wooden Ikea kitchen chairs. The small television on the counter that keeps Tang company during his otherwise solitary dinners is on. It's tuned to WSN. The network has been promoting the running of the Magnum Stakes for two weeks. Tang was known to place the occasional bet on the ponies, never anything big, certainly not anything like the potential payoff his involvement with Kong could provide. He picks up his list of potential candidates; every name has been crossed off.

Tang: "Maybe we can get away with placing the bets ourselves, and; if we pool our resources maybe we'll have enough to make it worthwhile?"

Lebow: "It's too dangerous. You got to assume that things could go sideways. We have to cover our asses. We need a buffer just like Michael Corleone."

Tang: "Who's Michael Corleone?"

Lebow: "You've never seen *The Godfather*?" Tang shakes his head. Lebow describes the scene in the movie when Senator Pat Geary asks mobster Willi Cici if he ever got a direct kill order from Michael Corleone or if Corleone used a buffer, Cici gives the Senator a half smile and answers *"Oh yeah… the family had a lot of buffers."*

Lebow: "We need a buffer." He tosses the list on the table, frustrated at their inability to come up with an appropriate partner.

Tang looks up at the television, Mattie Henry is interviewing John Paul, the jockey that just won the Magnum Stakes on board *Can't Dance Don't Ask Me*, paying a profitable twenty-to-one. His eyes focus on that luscious valley of flesh barely concealed by a soft creamy cashmere sweater that dips down between her perfectly displayed breasts. Tang points to the small television on the counter, "What about her?"

Lebow turns to look. "Mattie fucking Henry! She'd be perfect. Nobody will suspect her. And I hear she's the top paid female sport's broadcaster in the country. The rumor is she's a dame who likes the finer things in life, and she's not too picky how she gets them." Lebow and Tang have found their buffer.

A CUBE FULL OF SUGAR

12
A Cube Full of Sugar
Makes The Medicine Go Down

The afternoon's race broadcast is over and Mattie Henry thanks her video partner and producer. She goes to one of the automatic betting machines and cashes her ticket. Her thousand dollar investment paid a handsome return. The money goes directly into her Hancock account. She makes her way to the lounge figuring she'll have a celebratory Tom Collins before heading home. She spots Tommy Kong and Suarez enjoying a beverage at a table in the corner. They seem very pleased with themselves. She approaches, "You boys seem happy, somebody give you a hot tip?"

Kong: "It was a profitable day, thanks to you!"

Mattie: "Introduce me to your friend. I've seen him around the fronton a few times."

Kong: "Mattie Henry meet Antonio Suarez." Suarez waves a nonchalant hand in the air that passes for a greeting.

Mattie: "So Tommy... we got a deal? I clue you in at the track and you deal me in at the fronton?"

Kong looks at Suarez who answers for Tommy. "It was a nice gesture, you giving Tommy the tip on today's race. Can't say it wasn't a profitable afternoon, but we don't need any more partners. It's a company policy sort of thing, you understand I'm sure."

Mattie is steaming at their refusal to take her up on her offer. She's not used to getting turned down, and she doesn't like it. She just made these assholes a substantial profit and now they spit in her face. "Are you guys serious? I just gave you a big win and you tell me to fuck-off!"

Kong: "If it's fucking we're talking about, then perhaps we can work something out, otherwise we're not interested, that is unless you have another sure thing you'd like to share."

Mattie: "It will be a bloody cold day in Hell before I give you two schmucks the time of day." She dramatically wheels around on her six-inch dome pumps and heads for the exit. The two gangsters smile and enjoy the view as Mattie Henry strains the fabric of her tight skirt in an effort to escape the humiliation of getting metaphorically screwed.

In the video room that houses the security cameras that blanket just about every square inch of the Hancock Racetrack, Jesse James is going ballistic. Everybody in the room is turned facing her. "I want every fucking second of video from every fucking camera from five o'clock this morning until race time analyzed. You dummies better find out what the fuck happened. You're supposed to catch this shit before it happens, not after. We know that bitch was going to pull something, and we still didn't catch her. We look like a bunch of amateurs. That goddamn horse couldn't win that race if it was the only horse running. God Damn It! *Can't Dance Don't Ask Me* can't run worth a shit, let alone dance. Mattie Henry messed with the race and you better find out how. I want proof that she did this on my desk by tomorrow morning when I come in. Jesus Christ Almighty! Nobody! Fucking Nobody! Fucks with my racetrack!"

Jesse is almost apoplectic. She picks up an open water bottle from somebody's desk and flings it across the room. The security people all duck except for one guy who decided to text his girlfriend during Jesse's tirade. The bottle hits him in the chest, drenching him and his phone with water. The security guy looks wounded, "What the fuck?"

Jesse: "You want to file a complaint asshole? Come on, let's you and I go down and see Johnny Luck where you can voice your concerns about being abused by your one-hundred-and-ten-pound boss. Come on, let's go." The guy shakes his head.

Jesse: "Good decision. And as far as the rest of you numbskulls are concerned, find me the proof that that bitch pulled this off or else." Part of Jesse's display is an act, but part isn't. She knows this kind of thing happens around the track all the time but Carman warned her it was going to happen. Jesse warned security, and they still missed it. Her team looked like amateurs. As far as Jesse knew, Mattie Henry was a novice, and that pissed her off more than the actual scam itself. A deadbeat long shot and a couple of unlikely big payouts, it's bullshit, and Jesse is legitimately upset. She turns to leave mumbling to herself, "Fucking *Can't Dance*, the nag can't run either..." she continues to talk to herself as she heads back to her office.

THE CAMERA ANGLE

13
The Camera Angle

Jesse sits at her desk reading the report from her Chief of Security, Philip Cairns. Cairns is a fifty-year-old retired Marine Major. He sits and waits. He knows Jesse well and was not concerned about her tirade of the day before.

Cairns: "You kinda went a bit overboard yesterday with the guys. I don't think Billy will be texting his girlfriend any time soon when you're in the room."

Jesse: "Yeah, I guess it was a bit over the top, but Jesus Phil, we knew Mattie Henry was going to pull something and we still didn't catch her."

Cairns: "Look I don't blame you for being pissed. It's my job to stop this shit from happening, but we reviewed all the footage as outlined in the report and we found nothing unusual. Mattie Henry was seen on the video but that's not unusual since she was covering the race. The only strange item that came up was the position of the shedrow security camera. For some reason, it got knocked out of position and was faced in the wrong direction. Nobody noticed it until we reviewed the footage, but that could be a coincidence. Cameras get knocked around all the time; it's not unusual.

Jesse: "I don't believe in coincidences. Cameras magically get turned around, I don't buy it."

Cairns: "You know as well as I do that this stuff happens all the time. Jockeys use machines and hold horses; vets shoot up the animals with every substance known to man. You're never going to stop it. You can't. Besides, long shots win occasionally, especially when the times are as slow as they were yesterday."

Jesse: "There's something bigger going on here. Mattie Henry has been seen in the company of Tommy Kong and that means trouble. I figure they're pulling the same shit they did at the Miami fronton before we shut them down. You'd think they'd learned their lesson. Now it looks like they want in on the ponies. Mattie Henry seems to be the link between the Jai Ali and the track; that's what really concerns me."

Cairns: "I could have the guys hide some extra cameras and microphones at the fronton to keep an eye on Kong and Henry. See if we can pick up something? We could even wire the guy in charge of the private dining room, Bo Tang."

Jesse: "Bo Tang is the guy in charge of that dining room? Carman tells me he's been seen at the diner with Kong."

Cairns: "Everybody eats at Carman's place. People from the track and the fronton are bound to run into one another."

Jesse: "Again with the coincidences... I don't buy it. Bug the room and make sure Tang is covered. In fact, put a tail on him. Let's see who his friends are."

After the meeting with Cairns, Jesse makes her way out to the backstretch where she finds an elderly security guard sitting on a lawn chair reading *Fifty Shades of Grey*. Jesse is carrying two jumbo coffees. Jesse hands the older man one of the coffees. "Learn anything new from that book?"

The old man laughs. "Nah... I learned how to use a whip when I rode." The old man takes a swig of coffee. He knows Jesse wouldn't be there with coffee unless there was a problem. "Thanks for the coffee kiddo... what's up?"

Jesse: "Were you here yesterday for the Magnum?"

Pops: "Sure, everybody was on duty because of the big race."

Jesse: "See anything strange?"

Pops: "You mean anything that involves a horse that can't dance?"

Jesse: "You're still one sharp old jock, Pops."

Pops: "I figured you'd be curious about that."

Jesse: "I understand the camera got accidentally turned around."

Pops: "Nothing accidental about it. That cutie Mattie Henry was here with her cameraman taking video of the horses in the race, but she didn't pay much attention to *Can't Dance*. Not really unusual since it didn't appear to have a chance."

Jesse: "So who turned the surveillance camera around?"

Pops: "Mattie had the cameraman climb up and turn it. Nobody paid much attention. We just figured it was interfering with their taping. It was mayhem around that time. Everybody was getting ready for the race. I guess the guy forgot to turn it around when he finished shooting Mattie giving the horses their treats."

Jesse: "You saw Mattie Henry giving out treats?"

Pops: "Sure! She's always got a pocket full of sugar cubes for the horses. The guys even call her Sugar Henry."

Jesse sticks her hand in her pocket and pulls out five twenties. She tries to hand them to Pops. He waves them away. "No need sweetie, just doing my job, besides I should have had somebody check on that camera. Guess I'm getting old."

Jesse: "Nonsense. This place would fall apart without you." She insists he takes the twenties. "Buy yourself a new whip to try out some of the stuff in that book."

Pops: "I just might do that my dear... I just might." He gives Jesse a stage wink.

FOLLOW THE BOUNCING BO

14
Follow The Bouncing Bo

Mattie Henry sits in a chair in front of a large mirror. Linda, the WSN hairdresser assigned to the Jai Alai broadcasts, adjusts Mattie's hair so that it comes over her shoulders in the front. "What do you think? If you wear it this way, it frames your face."

Mattie: "You think?"

Linda: "Follow the line, Honey." Linda moves her hands down Mattie's chest, gently cupping her breasts. "You want to highlight your best features don't you?"

Mattie sees that the strands of hair point directly to the crease created by the soft mounds of flesh visible between the deep v-neck-opening created by the Scottish cashmere sweater she's chosen to wear on camera.

Mattie: "Yeah, I like it."

Linda: "Oh… I almost forgot. One of the guys in the dining room left a note for you." She hands Mattie a sealed envelope with Mattie's name neatly written on the front. Mattie is used to getting letters from fans, and occasionally even colleagues. Most are harmless, some are funny, and a few are unsettlingly bizarre. She keeps them all including, marriage proposals, death threats, and Polaroid's of body parts, just in case she ever decides to write her memoirs. Dressing provocatively certainly attracts the more peculiar elements of society, but as far as Mattie is concerned, it's the cost of doing business. She's been criticized by some of her female cable news contemporaries for dressing like a high-priced hooker, but as far as Mattie is concerned, until they start showing up on television dressed in Fran Lebowitz look-alike outfits, they best keep their opinions to themselves. Mattie opens the envelope and reads:

Private and Confidential
For Ms. Henry's Eyes Only

Miss Henry – My name is Bo Tang and I'm in charge of one of the private dining rooms at the Hancock Fronton. I believe I have come across some information that I think you'd be interested in. I understand you may think this strange and I'm sure you get your share of unwanted solicitations but I assure you this is a serious matter. If you're interested meet me at The Molly House at midnight tonight. – Bo Tang

Linda: "Anything wrong?"

Mattie: "I don't know. You know this Bo Tang fellow."

Linda: "I've seen him around, but no, I really don't know him. I think he's in charge of the dining room where that huge Chinese guy with the white Fu Manchu hangs out."

Mattie: "Thanks. Do me a favor?" Mattie takes her purse and rifles though it to find her wallet. She looks over both shoulders to see if anybody else is in the room. Linda looks as well. No one else is there. Mattie takes fifty bucks out of her wallet and hands it to Linda. "Nobody gave you a note, understand?" Linda nods agreement and stuffs the fifty bucks in her bra. Mattie holds up the folded note. "This never happened." Linda runs her finger over her lips signifying her lips are sealed.

THE MOLLY HOUSE

15
The Molly House

Bo Tang and Terry Lebow stand at the bar waiting for Mattie Henry to arrive. The Molly House could easily be mistaken for a nineteenth-century sitting room except that it had a large mahogany bar that stretched the length of the room. What appears to be men and women are lounging on over-stuffed chenille chairs and chaise lounges, drinking, talking, and what euphemistically could be called making-eyes-at one another. In addition to the obvious wanton ogling, there is lots of handholding and touching of a quasi-intimate nature. Tang didn't quite catch on immediately, but the more he looked around, the more he felt something was strange. He wasn't sure, but some women looked like they had five o'clock shadows while others appeared to have prominent Adam's apples.

Tang takes a sip of his screwdriver. "What kind of place is this?"

Lebow: "It's a men's club of a sort."

Tang: "So everyone here is a man?" Lebow nods.

Tang: "You like this kind of thing?"

Lebow: "Different strokes, for different blokes."

Tang doesn't know what to say. He's saved from saying something stupid or inappropriate by Mattie Henry's appearance in the lobby. The somewhat effeminate and officious maitre d' points to the bar where Tang and Lebow are sitting.

Mattie reconnoiters the environment as she makes her way through the crowded club to her potential co-conspirators. She approaches Tang, "You must be Tang." She looks at Lebow, "Who's this?"

Lebow: "I'm Terry Lebow."

Mattie: "Interesting place."

Tang: "Terry thought this is a safe place to meet. None of our colleagues have been known to frequent this kind of establishment."

Mattie looks around at the obvious all-male customers in the room. She smiles. "I see what you mean." The bartender arrives and Mattie orders a Rye and Ginger. Lebow pays. She looks at Tang. "You work Tommy Kong's dining room…" She looks at Lebow. "So what's your story?"

Lebow: "I'm in charge of the pari-mutuels at the fronton."

Up to this point, Mattie thought this whole setup was a joke that her male WSN colleagues were attempting to pull off, but now she was getting interested. If these two weirdoes had a way to screw Kong and Suarez and make some dough at the same time, then she was all in. Tang and Lebow spend the next twenty minutes describing the MBC operation and how they want to piggyback onto their plan. Their problem is, they're both too close to the operation, and neither one thinks they have a large enough bankroll. They need someone that can place the bets and put up some money. Mattie listens carefully to everything they say.

Mattie: "Nothing would please me more than to screw Kong and Suarez, but…"

Lebow: "Oh, you don't understand. We don't want to screw them; we just want to follow their lead so we can make a few bucks. You don't want to fuck-around with those guys. They find out we messed up their bets, we could all find ourselves waking up dead."

Mattie thinks for a second. She responds absent-mindedly while still mulling over the possibilities in her mind. "Waking up dead, ah… that would be a trick. How much cash do we need and how much can you put together on your own?"

Tang: "I got twenty-five hundred I can invest."

Lebow: "Same here, I'll come in for twenty-five hundred."

Mattie: "That's great! I can add another twenty-five hundred for my share. That gives us a seventy-five hundred stake. That should be enough to get us off the ground. You got to be smart about these things. These guys are dangerous. If we start small and build slowly, the likelihood of them catching-on to what we're doing is minimized. We need to pick our shots and only bet when the numbers make it worthwhile. When can you get me your money?"

They talk for another half an hour planning the details of their operation. By the time Mattie Henry leaves The Molly House, everything is arranged. As Mattie gets into her car to drive home, she's very pleased with herself. Tang and Lebow may be strange characters but they are the means for her to get even with Kong and Suarez. She plays the scenario over and over in her head. With a few small adjustments to the plan, she could come out way ahead, and if her wannabe partners somehow fall through the cracks and wake up dead as Lebow so quaintly described, then, *them's the breaks.*

EVERYBODY'S GOT A PLAN

16
Everybody's Got A Plan

Gebara has been in the Jai Alai game his whole life; he started playing as soon as he was big enough to strap a mini homemade cesta to his hand. His father and his uncle were both well-known Jai Ali players in Spain and Xavier followed in the family tradition. He knew every player in the league; he knew their strengths and their weaknesses, including those personality failings that could be corrupted. He knew first-hand the consequences of rejecting the game-within-the-game; consequences that ended his career when he impaled a hundred-year-old Banyan Tree with his brand new Audi.

According to the police report, the brake lines were cut. Gebara knew why it was done and who was responsible, but in Miami, Tommy Kong and Antonio Suarez were untouchable; healthy contributions to the right elected officials, guaranteed the police report would turned yellow with age before anyone even looked at it. In the end Xavier Gebara is lucky to be alive.

Gebara is happy with his new broadcasting gig, in a new city, in a revamped league that appears to be more willing to police the flaws of morally ambivalent athletes, despite his employer's reputation for cutting corners, as well as a few throats. Unfortunately, he could see the same corruption that poisoned the Miami fronton creeping into the Hancock operation. He wasn't surprised. As soon as he heard Kong and Suarez had basically taken up residence in one of the private Hancock boxes, he knew it was only a matter of time. And it didn't take long for the Fu Manchu moustache and *El Astronauta* to zero in on Urbina and Ola, a couple of young hotshots on the make, with expectations of living the Hollywood dream.

Gebara didn't know exactly how he was going to get revenge on Kong and Suarez for ending his playing career, but if he could find some evidence, he could take it to Jesse James. From what he heard, she didn't take kindly to people messing with her racetrack or her husband, financier, art dealer, William Stone, the man who ostensibly owned the league. Gebara like many of the Hancock Jai Alai employees hung out at the nearby Oasis Club. Xavier liked to party as much as the next guy, but positioning himself at the bar also gave him an enlightening view of the comings and goings of certain key individuals.

He was surprised when Kong and Suarez visited Solo and Mendoza at the club in one of the private party rooms. The meeting most certainly wasn't about fun and games as they immediately expelled the women as soon as they arrived. And from the look on the women's faces when they left, they were not pleased. When Mendoza got hammered by Ola, he knew right then and there that Solo and Mendoza turned Kong and Suarez down; it seemed the two gangsters found willing partners in the young and impatient Zarion Urbina and Iker Ola. Mendoza was lucky they didn't cut his brake lines, otherwise his injuries could have been a lot worse.

Gebara thought about approaching Solo and Mendoza, who he was sure would be willing to inflict some kind of retribution, but he decided their careers were already in jeopardy, so why drag them deeper into a La Brea Tar Pit of vengeance. He decided to take his concerns to Jesse James. Unbeknown to Gebara, Solo and Mendoza were already planning their revenge.

Early Monday morning Xavier Gebara shows up at the executive offices of the Hancock Entertainment Corporation. When Jesse James arrives, he is ushered into her office. After some initial 'hello how are you' small talk, Gebara gets to the point.

Gebara: "I'm sorry to be the one to tell you this but Miami is starting all over again."

Jesse: "You mean Kong and Suarez?" Gebara nods. Jesse continues, "I'm not surprised. That fucking Kong has got a head like a Teflon frying pan, no matter how many times you smash it against the wall, it just won't dent."

Gebara smiles. "You don't cook much do you?"

Jesse: "Not really... why?"

Gebara: "I think Teflon is known to be non stick, not non-breakable."

Jesse: "Yeah well you get my point. You know someone tried to kill that bastard by blowing up an entire building. Almost took out the entire block, but that asshole survived sitting on the crapper taking a nice peaceful dump surrounded by carnage."

Gebara: "I figure Kong and Suarez are working with Urbina and Ola to fix the matches. Maybe, they even got some inside help but I don't know that for sure. It looks to me like Solo and Mendoza turned them down. Mendoza's injury was no accident. If they're allowed to continue with this bullshit they're liable to bring the whole league down. I thought maybe you were the person to talk to about this."

Jesse: "I appreciate that Xavier. You did the right thing by bringing this to me. Leave it with me and I'll figure something out."

Gebara: "Thanks Jesse, I knew I could talk to you. It's not just about the job. I know your husband has a lot of dough tied up in this operation and I'd hate to see that go down the drain because of a couple of shitheads like Kong and Suarez."

Jesse: "You let me worry about Kong and Suarez, their time will come, but in the meantime I need you to keep an eye on that bitch you work with. I think she's involved. Not that I care if she ends up looking up to catch sight of the back side of dirt, but the Hancock doesn't need that kind of publicity."

Gebara: "I think you're right. She seems very interested in the wrong people and I doubt it's her journalistic instincts."

After some further discussion Gebara leaves. Jesse buzzes her secretary. "Get me Cairns on the phone." A few minutes later the phone on Jesse's desk rings. It's Philip Cairns. "Phil, call the tailor, I need to have a meeting tonight at my place."

Nine o'clock that night Philip Cairns and Mo Fields arrive at Jesse and Stone's condo to decide on a plan of action.

PICKING A WINNER

17
Picking A Winner

It is Champions' Week at The Hancock and LA is abuzz with gambling fever. Benny Silver came up with the idea of creating a week-long gambling extravaganza that would combine the IJAL Championships with the inaugural IJAL Mile for three-year-olds, and the IJAL Poker Championship. WSN has been promoting the week-long orgy of wagering insanity for months. The top-rated eight Jai Alai players and teams from across the IJAL network are invited to compete. The winning doubles team will share a grand prize of one million dollars while the singles champion will take home a cool million all for himself. Vegas jumped on the event like a lifer with a conjugal visit. Money poured in from all over the country. The betting pools were approaching record amounts making for a big potential payday.

Unlike Kong and Suarez who are in it for the long haul, Mattie Henry wants one big payoff. It's important for the MBC to keep a low profile, so their plan is to use intimidation and payoffs to influence the results just enough for them to gain a significant but plausible percentage advantage, but Mattie wants to get in and out quickly. As far as Lebow and Tang are concerned, they're flying by the seat of their pants just hoping to shadow the professional gamblers in order to make a few extra bucks. Unlike Mattie Henry who has her sights set on big numbers, Tang and Lebow are small-minded men with limited ambition, and even more limited imagination.

Mattie's plan is simple but not without danger. The key to a big payday is the size of the exotic wagering pools and the number of people who hold winning tickets. Money is pouring in from all over North American due to the massive amounts of publicity and advertising done by WSN and the Hancock. Mattie needs to pick a series of exotic wagers that few if anybody else will bet on.

To ensure she has the winning tickets, she intends to inject her favorite sleepy-time narcotic, Xylazine, into the energy drinks of the most likely winners without anyone noticing. Therein lies the danger; how to get the drug into the favorites' so their performance is slowed down just enough to give her picks the edge they need to win. Like most professional sports, all Jai Alai players are good, or they wouldn't be in the league. There is little to separate the best players from the worst, meaning, on any given day, anyone can win.

All Mattie has to do is tilt the odds in her favor. She has five grand of Tang and Lebow's money to play with. She has no intention of investing her own cash or placing the bets given to her by her so-called partners. They'll chalk their losses up to bad luck and go away quietly with their tails between their legs, while she walks away with a small fortune, or at least, that's the plan.

Mattie heard the scuttlebutt about Jesse James going ballistic about the *Can't Dance* situation, but to date, nothing has come back on her, so she figured she's in the clear. In fact, the situation is working out even better than she hoped.

Jesse will be so concerned about someone pulling something in the IJAL Mile at the track that she'll probably completely ignore the Jai Alai. Now Mattie has to decide which player is the most unlikely winner, the one everyone will stay clear of betting on. Even the most unlikely winner will have a few long-shot bettors in their corner but her plan is to stay clear of the Win, Place, and Show bets, and go with the more profitable exotics. As it happens, one player turns out to be the perfect target.

Gorka Mendoza is the key to Mattie's plan. He's been out of action since being hit by Zarion Urbina. Mendoza only qualified for the championship under a special injury exemption that states: *players cannot be discriminated against because of injury, upon their return, they will be posted eighth for both singles and doubles matches.* This gives Mendoza a pass for missing so much time, but an eighth-place posting almost guarantees he can't win; a player or team posted eighth has the fewest chances to win points because they are likely to play the fewest number of games and therefore will have difficulty in achieving the required number of points. To make matters worse the number of points needed to win the singles championship has been increased from the normal seven or nine to twelve.

That said, there are always people willing to put a few bucks on a long-shot. Unfortunately or fortunately, depending on where you sit, Mendoza is also rusty and not in game shape. His chances of winning the singles or helping Solo win the doubles is little and none. Even Mendoza's mother would have to think twice before placing a two dollar wager on such a guaranteed loser, making him the perfect key to winning a big pool.

Anyone who follows the sport understands Mendoza is the dog in the race. Even the casual bettor whose jumped on the Champions' Week bandwagon has at least watched the sports and news coverage which has widely publicized the statistical analysis in the IJAL Newsletter, an analysis put together by Terrance Lebow, Head of Pari-Mutuel Wagering, that places Mendoza as a 'do not bet' entry.

This would seem to make Mendoza the perfect target for Suarez and Kong to drop their money on, but the word from Lebow is they're afraid Jesse James and her Hancock brothers will smell a rat. Their choice seems to be Bolivar Solo who has fallen significantly in the rankings due to

Kong and Suarez's intimidation: a year-long effort to set up a season-ending big payday. Even with the low ranking and smart money aversion, no one will question a Solo's win, and no will suspect the fix was in. Now, all Mattie had to do is find a way to inject Xylazine into everyone's energy drink; everyone except Mendoza's.

A GIRL'S BEST FRIEND

18
A Girl's Best Friend

Champions' Week is a major success with unparalleled wagering interest approaching college basketball's year-end extravaganza. Television viewership is off the charts, making WSN, Benny Silver, William Stone, and their Hancock allies very happy. Stone's initial investment has doubled in value and the Hancock's revenues have soared. Jai Ali is an unexpected major hit. The Sunday night finale of Champions' Week is the Single's Championship with Zarion Urbina the odds-on favorite after a breakthrough season silently aided by the not so delicate hands of Tommy The King Kong and Marco Antonio *El Astronauta* Suarez.

Urbina and his partner, Ola, won the Double's on Saturday making them the favorites for the single's championship. They are posted first and second. Bolivar Solo has dropped down to sixth posting after an uncharacteristically poor season due to Mendoza's injury and MBC intimidation. Gorka Mendoza is posted last.

It's three AM Sunday and Mattie pulls into the empty Hancock Fronton parking lot. She checks her oversized handbag to see that she's brought her trusty bottle of Xylazine and the leather pouch containing the needed syringe. She knows the Palco de Pelotaris valet places six bottles of energy drink in each of the player's open lockers the night before every match. Each player has their favorite flavor, so it's unlikely they'll be any swapping. She looks at herself in the rear-view mirror, applies a fresh coating of gloss to her lips giving them an inviting shine that begs to be kissed. She adjusts the mirror down to get a better angle to see if her chosen cashmere sweater dips far enough to do its job. She cups her breasts, pushing them up and out to add that extra visual touch that says 'glad to see you.' She gets out of her car and heads for the Employee's Only entrance. She's greeted by a young security guard who recognizes Mattie's familiar twins from twenty feet away. He waves. "Is there a problem Miss Henry? Is there something I can help you with?"

Mattie: "No Charlie, I'm good. I left my phone in the players' room when I interviewed Zarion and Iker last night."

Charlie: "You want me to go with you to look?"

Mattie: "Thanks Charlie, but I know exactly where I left it. I'll just grab it and get out of your hair lickety-split."

Charlie: "Sure thing Miss Henry. Just let me know if I can be of any help."

Mattie: "You're a doll, Charlie." She gives him a kiss on the cheek, making sure her freshly exposed cleavage brushes up against the young security guard's arm. "And Charlie, if anybody asks, I wasn't here. I don't want people to start thinking I'm some kind of ditz leaving my stuff all over the arena. You understand... don't you Charlie?" The kid is melting into a puddle of male hormones before her eyes.

Charlie: "Of course Miss Henry, anything you say."

Mattie: "Thanks Charlie, you're the best." She gives him another peck on the cheek. "We're pals, Charlie, call me Mattie." She winks and heads for the players' room.

When she gets to the locker room she gets to work quickly. She doesn't have a lot of time and she doesn't want her new pal Charlie to get curious or decide he needs to be extra helpful. She quickly injects every pelotari's energy drink with Xylazine, everyone except Gorka Mendoza. Now all she has to do is place her bets.

YOU BET YOUR LIFE

19
You Bet Your Life

Mattie gets back to her condo by four AM and gets a couple hours of sleep. She gets up earlier than usual and heads out of town to an OTB in Anaheim where she'll have breakfast and place her wagers. It's Sunday so the traffic to Anaheim is terrible but not horrendous like during the week. She heads straight for a twenty-four-hour pancake joint across the street from the OTB that is licensed to take Jai Alai wagers.

Kong and Suarez set-up the entire season to push Solo down in the standings so that the odds on him will be high when it comes time for the big finale. He is the key to the MBC gang getting a substantial return on their investment. They plan on re-investing their winnings on Solo each time he plays until they ultimately dump all their pro-ceeds on a Solo-Urbina-Ola Championship Trifec-ta. While Kong and company are betting on each individual game plus the final results, Mattie is concentrating only on the Championship.

The key to her big payday is Gorka Mendoza, the man considered a wagering pariah by everyone including Kong and Suarez. With everyone but Mendoza slowed by the Xylazine sedative, she all but guarantees Mendoza will finish either first or second. You never know about these things; maybe someone decides they're not thirsty, but that is highly unlikely since athletes need to continuously hydrate.

Mattie's drug plan allows her to avoid scrutiny by not directly colluding with the players. Kong and Suarez will go crazy when they lose, but they won't suspect her. The players will take the heat. There's no drug testing in Jai Alai like in horse racing so that aspect of the scam isn't an issue.

The Hancock, Jesse James, and her boss, Johnny Luck won't care who wins as long as the Championship is a success. In the end, upsets happen, and Mendoza does have a track record as a winner. Everyone will assume his injury was overblown.

For the scheme to work, Mattie needs to use a wheel betting system. She needs to spread her cash out over a series of Quinella and Exacta bets that involve each of the other pelotaris, and Mendoza either finishing first or second in the Quinella and first in the Exacta. To cover all the possible winning wagers, Mattie has to purchase fourteen Exacta tickets but only seven Quinella tickets.

The Trifecta is different. It requires that you pick the top three finishers in order, making the betting process a lot more complicated. Mattie is counting on Mendoza finishing first, but she has no idea who will finish second and third.

To cover all the possibilities, she needs to purchase one hundred and twenty-six Trifecta tickets. She can only lose if Mendoza doesn't finish first. In total, Mattie has to purchase one hundred and forty-seven two-dollar tickets.

Since the payoffs for exotic bets aren't based on odds but rather on the size of the pot and the number of winning tickets that will split the pot, she only has to invest in two-dollar tickets for a total investment of two hundred and ninety-four dollars. That leaves her forty-seven hundred and six dollars to play with on individual game bets. Knowing that all the players except Mendoza are drugged allows her to wait for Mendoza to play and dump everything on him.

At this point, the only thing that could go wrong is Mendoza could get reinjured, or perhaps, run out of gas because he's not in top playing shape. Her chances of making multiple big scores are better than good. And if everything goes sideways, it's no big deal, after all, the money is Tang and Lebow's, not her's.

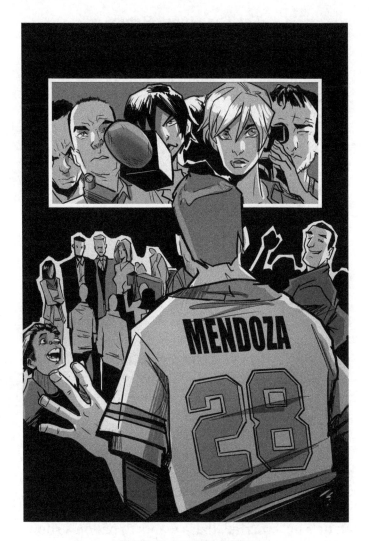

LET THE GAMES BEGIN

20
Let The Games Begin

The Hancock Fronton is the place to be for Sunday night's Single's Championship. Celebrities strut their stuff as they walk down the red carpet stopping only to talk to Mattie Henry on camera to promote their latest movie and tout their freebee designer threads provided by fashion's elite, hungry for the spotlight and star association. With everyone seated and the initial wagers placed, the games begin.

Mattie and Gebara announce the matches in an alternatively excited and breathless manner, conveying the overt and underlying tension inherent in the event. Mattie doesn't have to try too hard to get excited; she anticipates a big payday. The Kong-Suarez game plan plays out for the first few games with Urbina easily disposing of his doubles partner Iker Ola. He follows with an easy win over Samson Loyola, but finds he's lethargic and having trouble concentrating.

In between matches Urbina downs one full bottle of Xylazine infused energy drink, hoping that it wakes him up. He feels drugged, but he knows everyone but Solo and Mendoza have been paid so he's not worried. Ibara wants to put on a show even though he knows he is supposed to lose. He also doesn't feel great but avoids drinking any more energy drink. He makes a nice carombola shot that he figures Urbina will have no trouble returning, but Urbina slips as he tries to climb the wall to return the pelota. He lands awkwardly and twists his ankle badly. He needs to be helped off the cancha, It's unclear if he can return. Kong and Suarez are furious. They send one of their men down to the players' room to check on Urbina's status, but he's barred from entering by security.

Kong grabs Tang by the collar and rams him up against the wall like it's his fault Urbina got hurt. He demands more information from Lebow but Lebow can't get into the players' room either. Kong and Suarez start shouting conflicting instructions to Tang who is getting confused. He's trying to place their bets, text Mattie Henry, and relay Lebow's statistics, all at the same time.

In the broadcast booth Gebara looks over at his partner's cell phone; it's flopping on the table like a traveling salesman with an endless supply of quarters on a motel vibrating bed. Mattie is standing as she excitingly comments on Gebara's play-by-play. During a commercial break, she turns to Gebara, "This is better than sex." Gebara isn't so sure.

At the end of round one, Urbina is tied with Solo; each has two points; Ibara, Zabala, and Mendoza, each have one. During a short break before the start of round two when the points double Kong and Suarez argue, but they're not out of it yet.

Their Trifecta wager requires Solo, Urbina, and Ola to finish one, two, three. Urbina and Solo are tied with two points each, so they figure they're still in good shape. Ola doesn't have a point but there's still time for him to earn enough points to come in third; it all depends on how many matches he gets to play.

Even with the fix in, the matches may not favor their bet. Their major concern is Urbina's injury. They have enough Quinella and Exacta bets laid down to cover themselves, but the big money payoff needs a positive Trifecta result. If Urbina can continue, they should be fine. With everyone but Solo and Mendoza paid-off, Solo should have no problem coming in first. As far as Mendoza is concerned, they assume he's not a factor, but Urbina needs to continue to finish second, and Ola has to start winning some points to finish third. Everything is up in the air.

Round two starts with Mendoza destroying Ola and Loyola. He's playing like a man on a mission and Kong and Suarez are getting very nervous. Mendoza now has five points and Urbina is his next opponent. Everyone in the fronton including Kong and Suarez hold their breath waiting to see if Urbina will come out for his next match.

They start to bicker with one another about what to do. They are interrupted by a thunderous explosion of cheers that erupts from the crowd. Shouts of ZEE!, ZEE!, ZEE!, Zarion Urbina's nickname, ring through the fronton encouraging their new hero; the man that most of them have bet on to win.

Urbina does a couple of deep knee bends and bounces up and down once or twice to assure the crowd he's completely recovered, but his ankle hurts and his mind is foggy from the Xylazine he's consumed. The match begins. It's an epic contest lasting more than five minutes with every style of shot played. But Urbina hasn't got the energy to put Mendoza away. Urbina shouts at Mendoza in an effort to get him to back off.

The crowd cheers thinking he's taunting his opponent. Mendoza executes a *dos paredes* carom shot by playing the pelota off the side wall first so that it ricochets off the front granite in an acute angle heading for the out-of-bounds area. The pelota bounces just inches inside the court. Urbina races towards the pelota that is heading for the screen that protects the fans. He makes a desperate dive and in one motion catches the pelota twists in mid-air and releases the shot, but it falls short of the front wall.

Mendoza watches as Urbina hits the protective screen landing on the hard wooden out-of-bounds floor in a heap. "Tanto Mendoza!"

Mendoza goes on to beat Ibarra, but loses to Zabala, who beats Elizondo, who loses to Solo. Round two ends: Mendoza has nine points, Zabala has five, Solo has four, Urbina has two, and Ibarra has one. In round three Solo starts racking up the points with each win accounting for another two points. He beats Ola, Ibara, and Loyola giving him ten points. His next opponent is his partner Mendoza.

They play a marathon match but in the end, the younger Mendoza wins giving him nine points. He needs twelve to win and his next match is Urbina, who needs to go on a tear if he's going to finish second as demanded by Kong and Suarez. Urbina can hardly stand up. His ankle hurts and he's having trouble keeping his eyes open. He is not much of a match for Mendoza, who also finishes off his last opponent without too much trouble. Mendoza is the surprise IJAL Champion and winner of the one million dollar prize. His partner Bolivar Solo finishes second and Zabala finishes third. Kong and Suarez are shit-out-of-luck. When all is said and done Mattie walks away with one hundred and ninety-six thousand, four hundred and sixty-eight dollars; not a bad day's work. Kong and Suarez are cleaned out and they are not happy.

A TEA PARTY

21
A Tea Party

It's late and Benny Silver is tired. He sits quietly leafing through a copy of *Architectural Digest* that Mattie Henry has left on her coffee table. Her apartment has been professionally decorated with a classic mix of Bauhaus leather, chrome, and glass. There are sounds of tea being made in the kitchen. Silver hears the key being inserted in the front door. Mattie Henry enters surprised to see the light is on. She thinks she must have forgotten to turn it off when she left in the morning. She tosses her car keys in the Japanese bowl placed on the hall stand for just such a purpose. She walks into the living room and stops dead. She looks at Silver casually reading one of her magazines.

Mattie: "What the hell are you doing here?"

Silver: "Reading about some Italian billionaire's penthouse in Rome."

Mattie: "How the hell did you get into my apartment?" The sound of a kettle boiling and China mugs being rattled comes from the kitchen. "Who else is here?"

Jesse enters the living room carrying a white tray. On the tray are an Aldo Rossi Alessi teapot, a matching mug, two silver bowls of sugar, a bottle of Xylazine and a brown leather pouch containing a syringe. "Hey girl... we've been waiting for you. I made you a nice cup of tea. Have a seat." Mattie hesitates. Jesse places the tray on the coffee table and takes a seat on the couch beside Silver. "I mean it, have a seat. Now!"

Mattie takes a seat in the black leather Le Corbusier chair facing the coffee table. "Look... I can explain that stuff."

Jesse: "No need. We know why you have it, what you do with it, and how you know how to use it. Jesus girl... three professors, when did you have time to study?"

Mattie: "It's not what you think."

Jesse: "Sure it is, it's exactly what I think. I'll tell you the sad part. Benny here is an innocent, a civilian, just a guy trying to do his job. We never intended him to get involved in the more colorful aspects of our business, but then you decided to fuck with my race track. If that wasn't bad enough, you couldn't keep your hands off my husband's business, and nobody, fucking nobody, puts their hands on my husband's business but me. But I digress. Where are my manners?" Jesse pours some steaming hot tea into the mug. "How many sugars?" She looks up into Mattie's eyes. For the first time, she sees fear.

Mattie: "I'm really not thirsty."

Jesse: "I don't really give a shit. Have some fucking tea with sugar."

Mattie: "I'll take it plain, no sugar."

Jesse: "Oh you're going to have some sugar tonight, *Sugar*; that's what the boys around the barn call you, isn't it? Any idea why they'd call you that?" Mattie shakes her head. "Well tonight, you're having sugar, even if I have to shove it down your pretty throat myself."

Mattie: "You can't make me!"

Jesse looks at Silver. He hesitates. "Don't be shy Benny, some girls like it rough." Benny gets up and walks behind Mattie's chair. He puts his hands on her shoulders. She tries to shrug them off but his grip gets stronger, pushing her back against the soft leather. Jesse reaches down into her boot where she keeps her ever-present switchblade. She removes the pearl handle from the pocket incorporated into her custom Cuban-heeled boot. She presses the button and the six-inch stiletto pops out.

Mattie: "You can't do this."

Jesse: "Actually we can, and we are. I'll tell you what. Since you like to gamble so much, let's make it interesting. We have two bowls each containing sugar cubes: one bowl contains the cubes you dosed with Xylazine; the other is sugar straight from the box. You choose, maybe you'll get lucky." Jesse takes the blade and points to each bowl of sugar cubes.

Mattie nervously bites her lip. "I won't do it. I won't choose."

Jesse: "Okay, I'll let Benny choose for you. Which bowl, Benny?" She points the blade to each bowl once more.

Benny: "That one," indicating the bowl on the right. Jesse reaches for the sugar.

Mattie is near hysterical, "NO! Not that one, the other one."

Jesse: "You sure?"

Mattie: "Yes, I'm sure." Jesse reaches for the sugar from the bowl Mattie indicated. "No... the other one. The one Benny chose."

Jesse moves her hand over to the other bowl. She picks up a hand-full of sugar cubes. She drops one into the cup. She stirs the tea with a silver spoon from the tray. She drops another cube into the tea...

Mattie: "That's all, that's enough!"

Jesse drops two more cubes into the tea. "Whoops, my bad. Oh well, sweets for the sweet. My guess is, you'll really like it."

Jesse stirs the tea once more. She picks up the mug and walks around to where Mattie is sitting. "Open wide, Mattie dear." Mattie purses her lips tightly together, Silver's fingers dig into Mattie's shoulders. Jesse moves the mug close to Mattie's mouth. Mattie flings her head from side to side trying to avoid the inevitable. Jesse grabs Mattie's nose like it's the knob on top of a stick shift, she drives Mattie's head back against the leather. Mattie's mouth instinctively opens, gasping for air. Jesse dumps the tea down her throat and with her other hand caps her mouth so she has to swallow.

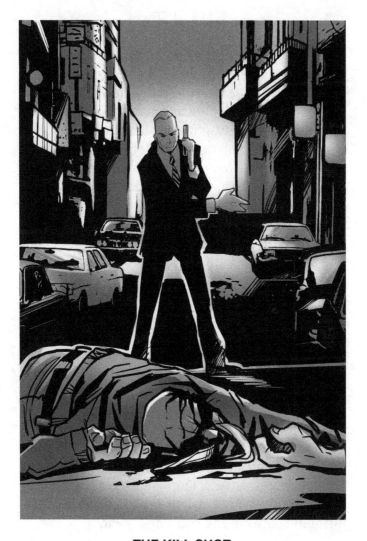

THE KILL SHOT

22
The Kill Shot

Philip Cairns sits at the end of the bar at the Oasis Club. It's been a while since he's done any real dirty work, but he knew when he took the job offered by Jesse that it was part of the job description. He absentmindedly feels for the Smith and Wesson tucked neatly under his custom Mo Fields' sports jacket. Unaware of Cairns' presence, Xavier Gebara waits at a table pretending to enjoy a watered-down Tequila. Neither man realizes the other is there.

The club is crowded with a varied mix of Hancock regulars and locals all enjoying a night on the town. Both men are fixated on the private room where Ola and Urbina are enjoying the company of a couple of female groupies. Standing outside by the double front doors of the Oasis is Max Chan, the club's valet, and a Hong Mian associate. Mo Fields, the tailor who moonlights as the Hong Mian's go-to zip, waits across the street hidden by the carved wooden cigar store Indian guarding the entrance to Ralph's Tobacco Shop. Fields holds his favorite Glock semi-automatic in his right hand. A black Cadillac Escalade pulls up in front of the club. Tommy Kong is driving with Antonio Suarez in the passenger seat.

Fields texts Cairns that the package has arrived. Kong and Suarez are there to meet Ola and

Urbina to find out what went wrong. They get out of the SUV and head for the front door. Kong tosses the keys to Chan and barks instructions, "No joyrides and don't scratch the paint!" He doesn't bother to look back to see if Chan is paying any attention. They enter the club and go straight to the private room where Ola and Urbina are partying. A few minutes later Cairns and Gebara notice two women exiting the party room, both women straighten their dresses as they head for a high traffic table to await their next celebrity conquests.

Cairns finishes his drink and pays his bill leaving enough of a tip that the bartender will unlikely remember he was there. Gebara pushes away the remains of the diluted alcohol distilled from the blue agave plant that surrounds the Mexican town of Tequila. Both men wait.

Ten minutes pass. Kong and Suarez come out of the private party room. Kong points to the two women they forced to abandon Ola and Urbina. Suarez shakes his head. Kong shrugs and both men head for the door. Gebara stands and follows. Cairns spots Gebara for the first time. Cairns moves for the door trying to avoid the throng of overly zealous customers. As he walks he texts Fields, *"Complication! Gebara is here. Abort?"* Fields responds, *"Negative!"*

Kong and Suarez exit the double front doors where Chan is waiting. Kong reminds Chan of their car, not that Chan needs any reminding. Chan leaves rounding the corner, heading for the parking lot down the street while Kong and Suarez wait on the curb. Fields steps out from behind the cigar store mascot and takes a step towards the curb immediately across the street from his targets. He slowly starts to raise his Glock. Kong and Suarez are sitting ducks. As Gebara is about to reach the front door of the club, a group of drunken partiers push past him piling out onto the street. The partiers pour out onto the sidewalk in front of the club, laughing and shouting as they say their goodnights. Fields lowers his gun as the club patrons head for the corner to find their vehicles. Kong looks up and sees Fields. He nudges Suarez as he points to Fields holding what looks like a gun.

Kong takes a step towards Fields. There's an odd almost whistling sound in the air. Kong collapses in a heap by the curb. Suarez looks down. Kong's skull has been shattered by a hundred and eighty mile-an-hour pelota. The Brazilian rubber hard-ball rolls between Suarez's feet. He starts to bend down to pick it up, but he never makes it. A second pelota strikes him in the temple. He collapses on top of Kong. Both men are dead from the force of the blows. Cairns and Gebara both exit the club just in time to see Kong and Suarez hit. Cairns looks across the road at Fields. Fields is pointing fifty yards down the street across from an alley. Bolivar Solo and Gorka Mendoza are standing in the middle of the road in street clothes with cestas strapped to their right hands. They wave the cestas in a salute. Gebara waves back. Solo and Mendoza disappear into the alley.

Chan, driving the Escalade, comes barrelling around the corner. He pulls up beside the bodies of Kong and Suarez. Fields heads across the street. Gebara bends down and picks up the two blooded pelotas. He turns to Cairns, "I'll help you get them in the car?" Chan hands Fields the keys to the car. He helps Cairns and Gebara stuff Kong and Suarez into the back of the Caddie. Several more club customers come out of the Oasis. They look at the three men finally getting Kong into the car beside Suarez. They comment on how some people just can't hold their liquor. They shake their heads in disgust and head for the parking lot around the corner. Kong and Suarez are safely off the street with Fields behind the wheel.

Cairns looks at Gebara, "What the hell were you doing here?"

Gebara: "Revenge." Cairns turns and heads down the street and around the corner where the Caddy is parked.

Cairns gets into the front passenger seat of the Cadillac. He looks at Fields, "Well that didn't go exactly as planned."

Fields smiles, "It rarely does."

EPILOGUE

23
Epilogue

Mattie Henry wakes up the following morning in bed. She has a massive migraine headache; she feels as if she's falling from a great height even though she's lying flat on her back. Her heart is pounding desperately as if it wants to escape her chest. The room is swirling around as if she's on a Merry-Go-Round. She tries to clear the cob-webs from her aching head but without luck. She attempts to sit up, but it takes too much effort. Was last night real or a nightmare?

She's cold. She peers under the covers. She's naked. She staggers out of bed. "What the fuck did they do to me?" The words ring in her ears, not realizing she's said them out loud. She re-members, "Xylazine... the bastards could have killed me."

She grabs a robe they kindly left on a nearby chair. She puts it on, shivering despite the fact it's warm in the room. She fumbles her way to the bathroom and looks in the mirror. She looks like shit. She feels something on her stomach, some-thing sticky. She opens her robe and looks down. A piece of paper is duct-taped just below her chest. She rips it off... "Fuck, that hurts!"

She reads: "*Next time you won't get a choice. Next time, it will be for real. PS – Deliver your winnings to Mo Fields C/O The Three Kings Tailor Shop by noon today."*

Meanwhile, Tommy The King Kong and Marco Antonio Suarez, *El Astronauta*, and their Cadillac Escalade are compacted into a nice neat cube at the Lakeshore Salvage Yard. Their remains will soon be incorporated into the future building-blocks of downtown Los Angeles's ever-expanding skyline.

Several Weeks Later

Terry Lebow and Bo Tang sit at the bar in The Molly House commiserating over the loss of their Mattie Henry investment and the cash cow that was Antonio Suarez and Tommy Kong.

A young man in his twenties takes the seat beside Lebow. "Can I buy you gentleman a drink?" Lebow assumes the young man is one of The Molly House regulars and he's looking to hook-up. "Sure why not? But you should know, my friend isn't into the molly scene."

The young man waves to the bartender at the other end of the bar. He points to the two Cuba Libres sitting in front of Lebow and Tang. He holds up three fingers signaling the barkeep to bring three more of the same. He sticks out his hand for Lebow and Tang to shake.

Lebow: "I'm Terry Lebow and this is my friend…" But before he can answer, the young man answers for him. "… Bo Tang." Lebow looks a little nonplussed, "You know who we are?"

Young Man: "I'm Freddy Gordon, and I have a proposition for you two gentlemen."

Watching from across the room are two well-dressed men sitting quietly in a darkened corner. Phil Cairns takes a sip of his Screwdriver. He looks at his friend. "Who's the third wheel?" Mo Field reaches into his custom suit jacket and pulls out a photograph and places it on the table in front of Cairns. "He's Freddy Gordon, Walter Gordon's kid."

Cairns: "Should we call Jesse? She could get Stone to back us up, or do we handle this ourselves?"

Fields: "I doubt these three will give us much of a problem. No point in getting Stone involved. I'll take Tang and Lebow. You handle Gordon."

Across the bar Lebow, Tang and Gordon seem all chummy. The new pals seem to have bonded over the prospect of resurrecting their money-making scheme. The three new pals get up and head for the door. Fields and Cairns follow.

The End

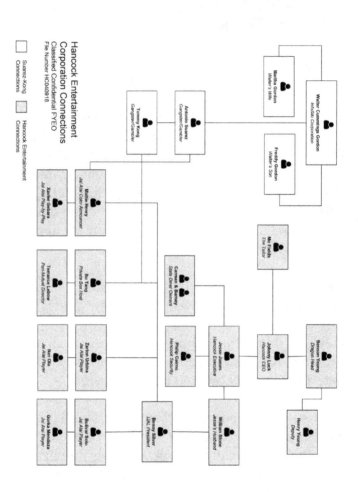

HANCOCK ENTERTAINMENT CONNECTIONS

Jai-Alai Glossary

Aro: The wooden frame of the cesta.

Arrimada: A reverse-spin shot that goes along the sidewall.

Atchiki: The interval between catching the ball and returning it.

Bote corrido: When a ball slides instead of bouncing.

Bote pronto: An underhand catch on a short hop. (Scoop)

Buzzball: A hard thrown shot.

Cancha: The court.

Carombola: A ball that hits the front and side walls, and then hits the cancha and bounces off in the direction of the screen.

Cesta: The "basket-racket".

Cestero: The person that makes or repairs the cestas.

Chaval de Pelotas: Ball boy

Chic-Chac: A ball that hits the floor near the back wall, then immediately hits the wall.

Chula: The ball hits the base of the back wall and returns without bouncing (it rolls instead).

Cinta: The cinta is used to tie the cesta to the player's hand.

Contracancha: The wooden outbounds area on the right side of the cancha.

Corredores: Bookmakers

Corta: An underhand serve.

Costillas: The ribs of the cesta.

Dejada: A soft shot that barely reaches the front wall and bounces off just above the foul line.

Delantero: The front court player. The back cour player is the **zaguero**.

Dos paredes: A carom shot that hits the front and side walls in any order. *Dos* means two and *paredes* means walls.

Efecto: The spin on the ball.

Equipo: A team of two pelotaris.

Faja: The sash worn around the waist of the pelotari.

Frontis: The front wall.

Fronton: The building in which jai alai is played.

Guante: The leather glove attached to the cesta.

Juez: Judge.

Lateral: The side wall.

Libre: If a player wants to signal his teammate move closer to the wall he will shout *libre*.

Mala: Shot out of bounds. *Mala* means bad.

Mimbre: The reeds of the cesta.

¡Mucho!: Fans shout of approval.

Palco de pelotaris: Where pelotaris sit while waiting for their turn to play.

Pared chica: The ball hits low on the back wall with a short bounce.

Partido: A match played to a fixed amount of points, usually 30 points.

Pasa: An overhand serve. The opposite of a *corta*.

Pelota: The ball.

Pelotari: A Jai Alai player.

Picada: An overhand shot thrown with a snap of the wrist creating a lot of spin so the ball hits high up the wall and bounces in a sharp angle.

Pica y vete: The ball hits the front wall, then bounces off the floor towards the player's box.

Rebote: A shot made-off the back wall.

Saque: The serve.

Scoop: An underhand catch on a short hop. (**Bote pronto**)

Tanto: The point.

Zaguero: The backcourt player. The front court player is the **delantero**.

Author Biography

Jerry Bader is Senior Partner at MRPwebmedia.com, a media production company that specializes in Web video, audio, music, and sound design. Mr. Bader has written and produced dozens of video commercials for clients. Writing scripts and novels is a natural extension that grew out of the experience of creating attention-grabbing mini movies that focus on the emotional motivator.

Mr. Bader has written over a hundred articles on marketing, and he's self-published marketing e-books, hybrid graphic novels, biographies, and a series of children's books. The Neo Noir Hybrid Graphic Novels are story concepts developed with the goal of having them turned into television series or feature films. There are currently ten screenplays, five of which have been self-published as hybrid graphic novels: *The Method, The Comeuppance, The Coffin Corner, Grist For The Mill* and *The Black Crane.*

He's also written *The Fixer* published by Rebel Seed Entertainment. It has consistently been in the top ten percent in several Amazon categories. *The Fixer* is based on the true-life story of a colorful horse racing character. The follow-up to *The Fixer* is *Beating The System* that continues the story of the horse racing legend. Mr. Bader has also written *Organized Crime Queens, The Secret World of Female Gangsters, What's Your Poison? How Cocktails Got Their Names, Cowboys, Lawmen, & Outlaws, The Outlaw Rider, Dead End, Palermo, Stone Cold, The Aussie Switch, Ballet of Bullets, Noir I, Noir II*, and the soon to be released: *Deception.*

Mr. Bader has also written a series of children's books, ZaZa Books For Kids, that currently includes, *Two Dragons Named Shoe, The Town That Didn't Speak, The Criminal McBride, The Bad Puppeteer, Mr. Bumbershoot, The Umbrella Man, The Ninth Inning,* and *14 Ridiculous Tales of Sage Silliness.*

The Outlaw Rider

by Jerry Bader
Illustrated by Paola Ceccantoni

THE OUTLAW RIDER

DEAD END

by Jerry Bader
Illustrated by Paola Ceccantoni

DEAD END

PALERMO

STONE COLD

THE AUSSIE SWITCH